S0-BXZ-945

Reap the South Wind

Other Five Star Titles
by Irene Bennett Brown:

No Other Place
Long Road Turning
Blue Horizons
The Plainswoman

Reap the
South Wind

Women of Paragon Springs Series #4

Irene Bennett Brown

Five Star • Waterville, Maine

PLYMOUTH PUBLIC LIBRARY
130 Division Street
Plymouth, WI 53073

Copyright © 2001 by Irene Bennett Brown
Women of Paragon Springs Book 4

All rights reserved.

This novel is a work of fiction. Names, characters, places and incidents are either the product of the author's imagination, or, if real, used fictitiously.

Five Star First Edition Romance Series.

Published in 2002 in conjunction with
Multimedia Product Development Inc.

Set in 11 pt. Plantin by Myrna S. Raven.

Printed in the United States on permanent paper.

Library of Congress Cataloging-in-Publication Data

Brown, Irene Bennett.
    Reap the south wind / Irene Bennett Brown.
        p. cm.—(Five Star first edition romance series)
    (Women of Paragon Springs ; bk. 4)
    ISBN 0-7862-2817-2 (hc : alk. paper)
    1. Women pioneers—Fiction.   2. Kansas—Fiction.
I. Title. II. Series.
PS3552.R68559 R43 2002
  813'.54—dc21   2001042853

~ Dedication ~

To my husband, Bob,
whose hard work, love, and encouragement
helps to keep my dreams aloft.

Chapter One

On that hot September day they came down from southern Kansas's Red Hills to the border town of Kiowa and found the place a'zither with people like a hill of ants. *We've come too late,* Lucy Ann thought, dismayed. She wasn't sure if she should feel sorry or glad.

She drove the bumping provision wagon behind their big brown team, Yance and Osage. The searing winds had loosened her ash-blond hair from its coronet of braids and she constantly brushed wisps from her eyes. Off to the side, her husband, Admire, rode his flashy bay-and-white pinto. Their daughter, Rachel, a comely, raven-haired young woman of twenty, sat swaying on the wagon-seat next to her mother. The Walshes were five days away from their old home at Paragon Springs, had camped near other land-hungry folk the night before on the banks of the shallow Medicine River.

Despite the many schooners and riders they'd seen heading in the same direction as theirs, Lucy Ann wouldn't have guessed that so many would already be *waiting* at Kiowa for the Cherokee Strip Run.

Making the Run with several of his friends was Admire's dream. They would take a claim each, a half-mile apart, near the Cimarron River. Together they would have a cattle spread the size none of them could ever own alone. It would be like Jack Ambler's vast Rocking A holdings back in Hodgeman County. They had all worked together there as cowhands when they were young, before that country was cut up into small, fenced farms by homesteaders.

She would like for Admire to see his dream fulfilled, but in her heart she knew that they ought not to have left Paragon Springs or sold their farm. The Run was such a gamble. She licked her sunburned lips; swallowed the dryness in her throat. The skin around her light blue eyes crinkled as she tried harder to see everything.

Spread out before them, centered by the tiny village of Kiowa, Kansas—average population seven-hundred souls—was a teeming mass, a vast encampment of thousands of human beings, hundreds upon hundreds of tents, wagons, and horses.

There was a pall of flying dust everywhere. The sun was scorching. Higher in the sky of boundless blue there wasn't a single cloud to give hope of rain. But heat and dust were not her biggest worries.

"Admire," she called out tentatively, "how can there be land enough in the Strip for all these folks? Many of them will have already registered for the Run."

He wore a deep frown but didn't immediately reply. Above his coal-dark beard, his black eyes were taking in every aspect of the situation laid out before them.

"Don't borrow trouble, Lucy Ann," he finally said, although that had never been her way. He pushed his dusty hat back from his perspiring brow. "Maybe we should'a come a week earlier, been first in line when they opened the registration booths. But I got this Chickasaw pony," he leaned forward to pat the pinto's neck. "He is as fast as anythin' that can fly. They'll still be givin' out certificates, Run hasn't started and it won't for another week. Come September 16th, I'll get us a good claim."

She wished she could be as sure. Kiowa was only one such point where home-seekers could register for the Cherokee Run. Other registration booths were located as well on the northern border of the Strip at the towns of Cameron, Hunnewell, Caldwell, and Arkansas City, Kansas. Booths on the southern border of the Strip were located at Stillwater, Orlando, Hennessey, and Goodwin, Oklahoma.

If there were this many folks camped at each place of registration, and many would have fast horses, then there was surely not enough land to go around, even though the Strip was said to be a six-million-acre parcel. That was an impressive amount that the government had bought off the Indians, but not land enough to provide 160 acres to each of the thousands gathering at the registration booths.

And that did not take into account the numerous Sooners who were reported to have sneaked into the Strip and who were hiding in the brushy ravines and gullies, ready to stake their claim on the instant, while other participants had at least a fifteen-mile ride to make after the starting gun sounded.

"I think Mama may be right," Rachel spoke up from beside Lucy Ann. "We shouldn't have ever left our farm back home. But if we do have to go back to Paragon Springs," she added with assurance, "there are good friends there who will take us in. They'll be glad to see us back."

Lucy Ann knew Rachel was thinking of folks at home who were as dear to them as true kin: Aurelia and her daughter, Zibby; Meg Gibbs and her family. Rachel's mind would be particularly on Aurelia's son, David, with whom she was in love.

"Not goin' back," Admire growled. "I ain't never goin' to be a farmer again. We're claimin' us a ranch in Oklahoma, gonna raise cattle and horses, and that's my final word. Now, follow me," he put the pinto into a trot out in front of their wagon.

Lucy Ann waved at the dust in front of her face, clucked

her tongue at the team. She turned to smile in sympathy at her daughter as they set to drive their way through the throngs of wagons and people. "David will come find us," she said softly, "and I don't think it will take him long, either."

Those last painful days before they left Paragon Springs, it had been obvious that David was deeply in love with Rachel. But it would take some doing for him to get over his shyness and take action, something he ought to have done ages ago. Rachel, a decent, proper girl, could only wait for him to do the asking.

It was needless to try to drive into the town proper where crowds were thickest. Admire, on the pinto, skirted the heaviest crowds and led them northeast of town where the camps thinned out. "We'll put up here," he said, halting at a spot where the sun-parched grass was less beaten, the dirt not so thick. He didn't mention that their original plan was for Lucy Ann and Rachel to have a hotel room or to stay in a boarding house in town where they would wait for him to make the Run. They all three now realized without discussion that folks in those places would be sleeping five abed, if beds in town were available at all.

"All right, Ad," Lucy Ann said quietly, weary and aching as she climbed down from the wagon. He didn't get down, but stayed in the saddle. She could see how much he wanted to be on about his business of registering for the Run and finding his friends. He needed to find out from them what their chances were with so many homeseekers already about. "Rachel and I can manage here," she told him.

He rode over to her, a grateful grin breaking across his dusty, black-bearded face. "If I'm not back in time, don't wait supper. It might take me a while to find Lofty Gowdy,

Bama, and the rest of 'em and learn of our chances."

When he was gone, she and Rachel set up their tent, rolled out their bed-blankets on a tarp inside, and unloaded cooking utensils. In that short length of time, three other wagons rolled in to set up camp near them and send an additional coat of dust over everything. One of the wagons was drawn by a pair of the scrawniest, flea-bitten-est gray mules Lucy Ann had ever laid eyes on. Their owner was a shifty-eyed, unkempt sort. What concerned her most about him was the knife in a sheath as long as a calf's leg that he wore from his wide belt.

The other folks didn't look so threatening and she gave them a reserved nod of greeting.

"Mama," Rachel said, when they had finished preparing their site for a long stay, "it looks like the Medicine River flows by over there." She pointed northeast at a tree-fringed wrinkle in the red bluffs. "It would be so nice to have water for a bath."

Lucy Ann agreed and they set off carrying buckets and a burlap bag to carry sticks and weeds for their supper fire. They had a small amount of fresh water back at camp that they had brought with them, enough to fix a meal or two. But she wanted plenty; they needed drinking water and so did the stock.

They came to the riverbank after about a mile walk. "Mama, look," Rachel spoke with heavy disappointment, "there's no water, the river is dried up!" Her pretty, olive-skinned face wrinkled into a frown. The searing winds whipped her pale blue skirts as her hand went up to cover her mouth.

They stood side by side looking down into the empty riverbed. The bottom was indeed dry; Lucy Ann's eyes followed huge ribbons of cracks, first one direction, then the

11

other. There was not a cupful of water in sight. "It's the drought," she said in a low, quiet voice, although Rachel knew the facts as well as she. "It was that way at home. I don't think I can remember the last time it rained, even a little shower. Most of the creeks and rivers have dried up from the heat we've had this summer."

"I wish we had never come here," Rachel said sadly. "We could have got by back home, somehow. All—all our friends are there." *David* is there, her stricken eyes said. She would have been available, when he got around to asking for her hand.

"Likely we could have gotten by," Lucy Ann answered, slipping her arm around her daughter's waist, "but coming here to make the Run is your father's last chance to have what he wants: a ranch, where he can go back to his natural work with cattle and horses. He never liked following the plow, planting, milking cows, and stone work; he did it for us. Now, we have to do what we can for him and his dream. We *owe* him, honey," she said.

It was a fact never far from Lucy Ann's mind that she and Rachel were beholden to Admire in ways they might never be able to repay enough.

Twenty years ago, Ad had left his job as a cowhand for Jack Ambler to marry fourteen-year-old Lucy Ann and become a farmer. He gave her his name and pledged to provide and care for her when most other men would have shunned her for what Sioux renegades had done to her months earlier in Nebraska.

Rachel was the result of that Indian outrage Lucy Ann had suffered. Once Ad was able to accept the truth of the conception, it was no-never-mind with him most of the time. He loved them both, as well as Lucy Ann's young brother, Lad. By making them his family, he felt he was atoning to his own mother for his inability to prevent her rape and killing by bushwhackers following the War Between the States.

Amazingly, Rachel looked like Ad. They were both dark, while Lucy Ann was fair, blond and blue-eyed. Only a few close friends in Paragon Springs knew of Rachel's true parentage. Rachel had known from the time she was small. She couldn't change the despicable facts of how she was conceived, but she could be as much like Lucy Ann as possible and she never stopped trying. She was kind, thoughtful, hard-working, a bit on the quiet side. Rachel had been an excellent school teacher in Paragon Springs. Where Admire Walsh was concerned, he was her one and only father, ever.

"Come Rachel," Lucy Ann took her daughter's hand, "we'll find water back in town. There will be families there with wells, they will let us have water."

They stopped at several homes in town, after pushing through crowds, only to be refused water or to be told it would cost them. They continued their search, disbelieving at first that they would have to *pay,* give up a portion of their slim funds for *water.* Where they came from water was something that was shared willingly with whomever was in need of it.

On their sixth try a harried resident explained, "We didn't ask all you folks to come here." He was a tall, thin man, his shirt was damp-dark with perspiration; wet curls were plastered to his forehead below his battered felt hat. He waved toward the myriad camps surrounding the town and the throngs crowding the small streets, "Our water supply hereabouts was low to begin with, due to the drought, then you all come. We shouldn't be expected to provide water, we scarcely have enough for our ownselves."

Lucy Ann nodded, "I understand." She had enough

water to fix supper, and maybe breakfast. But then there was tomorrow and the day after and the day after—"I will pay," she said, deciding there was nothing else she could do. He shook his head, as if angry at himself for relenting, but he let them have a bucket of water for three dollars cash.

Lucy Ann was so shocked at the price she couldn't talk, but she paid. On their way back to their camp, she told Rachel, "Papa won't believe I had to pay for water but we've got to have it."

Rachel nodded. Just trying to find water had made their throats too dry for talking.

When they reached their camp, they found six more outfits had pulled in and they were tightly surrounded; wagon-tongue to wagon-tongue, horse backside to horse backside.

"Dear heaven!" Lucy Ann whispered, "what's to become of this?" A loner in many respects, she had had all the elbow room she needed back on their farm. Their hometown, too, had felt spacious. She could be herself, not cramped, wherever she went. It was uncomfortable to have dozens of strangers bunched in around her until she felt she couldn't move or breathe. None of the people appeared friendly...

If she minded her own business, she decided, they would likely mind theirs and leave her be. Covertly taking in the situation, she saw that a few women in the other camps were wearily at work over their cook-fires. Their menfolk sat in the shade, chewing tobacco, spitting, and seeing to some small chore or other. Some of the men lay on the ground, sleeping. Doing her best to feel at ease, she nodded and smiled at the other women. She made her own skimpy fire and set about preparing the evening's victuals.

Rachel came from the tent with a pan of potatoes to

peel. They would also have prairie chicken fried in bacon grease—Ad had shot the bird earlier that day—and corn-bread. Lucy Ann wished they had greens, but the summer sun had long since seared every green living thing to a brown crisp.

Despite her private vow to mind her own business, it was impossible for Lucy Ann not to overhear discussions around her, particularly the loud arguments. There seemed to be a dispute about whether settlers could make the Run by train on railroads already built into the Oklahoma Terri-tory after the first Run, in 1889. She heard one man say that Interior Secretary Hoke Smith was going to allow trains to be used but that they could not travel more than fifteen miles an hour and would stop at points five miles apart.

She hoped the fellow was correct. Otherwise, the train riders would have unfair advantage over other vehicles and riders, like Ad and his companions.

After the sun went down, the temperature dropped sev-eral degrees and it cooled off. Rachel went inside the tent to read by lantern light. Lucy Ann remained in the dark by their small fire with her shawl wrapped tight around her and she was there when Ad rode in. She relaxed and felt safer, her relief slipping away when he told her that he couldn't stay, not even for the night.

He accepted the plate of food she'd kept warm for him, and told her as he ate, squatting by the fire, "The lines up to the registration booth have been there for days. Thou-sands of men and women are ahead of me, the line stretches two damn miles back! The land clerks is registerin' only about two-thousand folks a day. I got to get my place in line and stay there 'til the Run, but I wanted you to know."

He would have to be in line *night and day for nearly a week?* "Ad, how—are you sure—?" she started to ask, then she said, "Go ahead. We'll find you, we'll find the line in the morning. We'll bring you your meals and—water to drink. You won't have to leave your place. Don't worry about us here."

Rachel had come from the tent to sit quietly nearby.

"But I do worry," he said, looking around him into the dark at the other close campfires, the hordes of tents. "Watch your backs. I hear tell there ain't near enough food or water for everybody camped here. Stealin' is a danger. I know now that I should've left you two in Paragon Springs where you'd be comfortable, while I come on here to make the Run. I could've come back there for you after I got our land." He scowled angrily in the light from their fire.

"I wanted to be here with you, Admire Walsh, and I still do," Lucy Ann told him with feeling. This Run was his dream and even though for the most part she thought it could be a mistake, she would stand with him, be there when he needed her. She couldn't consider anything else. "Once you stake our claim," she told him encouragingly, "we won't have a long trip to our new place. By staying here, Rachel and me will be only a day's ride or so away."

He wanted to know that she had handy the old .44 pistol she had brought with her to Kansas years before. "I'll see that you have plenty of ammunition," he said. "I don't think you'll have call to use it, but you never know."

There was a time, after the Indian attack in Nebraska that took all of her family except her brother Lad—who had been partially scalped but lived—that she intended to use the pistol and her one bullet to end her life. Learning when she got to Kansas that there was no one else to take care of Lad, she had made the decision to stay alive for him. There

16

wasn't a day of her life since that she wasn't glad she'd made that decision.

"Rachel and me will be just fine, Admire, now you go on and do what you have to do."

Admire was not a demonstrative man. It wasn't easy for him to offer praise or put his feelings to words. So it was like a gift of pearls when he said in a husky voice, "You are a prize, Lucy Ann, the finest wife a man could ask for."

He hustled to the other side of the fire where their daughter sat on a blanket. He squatted down and put his hand on her shoulder. "Rachel, I'm sorry for us needin' to be here. I know that this place ain't to your likin' and you would've liked to've stayed back to home where David is. But I promise you, I will stake a fine claim, make a good home for you and your Mama. If your David has the good sense I think he does, he'll come to your new home and claim you."

"I know. Thank you, Papa." She reached up to pat his hand on her shoulder. She smiled at him in the light thrown from the campfire. He returned the grin.

Lucy Ann thought again how remarkable it was that Rachel had taken on Ad's gestures, his facial expressions, 'til a body would swear she was his own. Life did have its blessings in spite of suffering and hardships such as those facing them now.

Chapter Two

That first night Lucy Ann lay awake beside Rachel in the tent with the loaded .44 near at hand. With Ad staying at the line—she had remembered to send a bed-blanket with him—it was hard to sleep. Hour after hour she listened to the noise from the camps around them: explosive, violent arguments, drunken shouting and laughter, a woman's sobbing cry, and for a while even the discordant, sawing away at a fiddle, the drumming of a tub and what sounded like dancing.

Her head began to ache. She tried to push the pain away and have good thoughts about Ad and their future, the ranch he wanted. But that was nearly impossible. The dark feeling that they had made a terrible mistake in coming there seemed to have settled into the marrow of her bones.

It was going to be hard to hide her true feelings from him but she wouldn't shatter his hopes. There was a chance he could be right and the land he desired so much would be his. No matter what happened, she would be strong, stand by him, and help him all she could.

The night seemed a hundred hours long and she continued to toss restlessly. It must have been near dawn when she heard someone, or something, enter their tent. The sound was much closer than the carousing outside. Her eyes popped open and she lay rigid. It was very dark; she hoped the snuffling was from a stray dog finding its way inside their tent in a search for food. Her scalp crawled when she smelled the stink of a man, it was hard to breathe.

She started to rise and patted the ground around her in a

frantic, useless attempt to find her gun. A heavy human form crawled onto her bed, kneeing her, hands groping and catching at her. In an instant she was back in time: *the savages are at me again.* She recoiled as panic ripped her apart, her skin sprang an icy sweat. She screamed, but no sound came, only a tearing in her throat. Her mind reeled, rebelling against the pain and filth they would afflict on her again. *No!*

She exploded into action, a fiendish dervish. She thrashed and kicked, beat at flesh and bone with hard fists, yanked handfuls of hair, clawed his face. For seconds, or minutes, or a lifetime, she fought, heaving the heaviness from on top of her. She crouched over him, her fists finding him in the dark to pound at him with all her strength, over and over as he grunted and groaned unresisting and her hands began to catch in the blankets. "No! No!" she sobbed. "No!"

"Mama, what is it? Mama? Mama what's happening? What's wrong?" It was a moment or longer before Rachel's terrified voice penetrated Lucy Ann's wild determination, slowed her swinging fists in the gloom inside the tent.

Lucy Ann sat back on her heels in a daze. The man seemed to have passed out or maybe she had knocked him unconscious. She answered, her voice trembling and eerie, "There is a man in here, he must be drunk. I have him down. Light the lantern, Rachel."

"Mama!" Rachel exclaimed when she had struck a match to the lantern and held it up, throwing a circle of light around them inside the tent. She looked at Lucy Ann as she might at a madwoman.

Lucy Ann's hair was wild and loose, her nightgown was gathered up around her thighs as she straddled the intruder. "It's all right, Rachel," she said quietly. "Find the gun.

Then we can deal with whoever this is in here with us." She felt peculiar, not at all like her quiet, reserved self. But *this time* she had fought back and she had won. She took the gun from Rachel.

"Mama, what are you going to do?"

Herself again, she didn't really know. She couldn't shoot him. When he came around she could threaten him with what could happen if he ever came back. She could turn him over for punishment, if Kiowa had law enforcement, a sheriff. Considering all that was happening in the encampment that first afternoon and evening, she doubted there was any kind of law that would listen to her. There were soldiers present but they were there to keep order in the Run itself.

"Get away from him, Mama," Rachel ordered. "I don't think he's drunk, he looks very sick, to me."

For the first time, Lucy Ann took a good look at their intruder. Slowly, she crawled away from the gaunt, ragged man. She smoothed her nightgown down, knelt beside him. Slowly, she reached out and with the back of her hand touched his face. He was burning with fever. "Dear God, Rachel, you're right. I don't smell drink on him, just sweat—sickness. What've I done? And why did he come into our tent?"

"Maybe he was out of his head and in the dark got confused?"

Lucy Ann nodded. Of course Rachel was likely right. She felt terrible and hoped that she hadn't hurt him badly on top of his sickness.

Grabbing him by his scuffed, booted ankles, they pulled him outside. Lucy Ann put a rolled blanket under his head and a damp cloth on his forehead. She followed Rachel back into their tent where they both began to dress and decide what to do with the intruder.

Lucy Ann was fastening her braids into place when she heard voices outside. "That's Pa, all right," a young male voice said. A woman's voice answered, "He must've passed out over here by these folks' tent. Or, they was tryin' to do him harm! Did they rob him, d'ya think?"

Embarrassed and worried at the same time, Lucy Ann took her lantern and left the tent. A pudgy young man in patched overalls and torn shirt, and a giant, raw-boned older woman in faded calico were bent over the man Lucy Ann had dragged outside. The woman's face within the frame of her flyaway gray hair was creased with worry when she looked up at Lucy Ann.

"He got into our tent," Lucy Ann explained. "I'm afraid I hit him, but I'm not sure that I really hurt him. He is sick." She spoke with regret at the same time she realized that he could have been a bad sort bent on doing them harm and she was right to fight.

"We're sorry, Missus," the woman said. "My man, Elgin, took sick two days ago. He's been out of his head since yesterday morning. He must have gone out to relieve himself in the night, then couldn't find his way to the right camp. We're very sorry." The man began to stir and the woman said, "There, Elgin, there. You're all right."

Lucy Ann rushed forward to help the pair get the older fellow onto his feet. "I'm sorry I misunderstood—didn't realize until too late that your man is sick and was lost. Have you found a doctor for him?" The sun was just beginning to come up and she could see how bad off the man really was.

"We tried. Our luck thataway hasn't been good." The woman put an arm around her husband, her shoulder up under his arm. He sagged against her, but his bloodshot eyes were open. His skin was purplish with fever. He seemed oblivious to his surroundings, making Lucy Ann feel worse. The woman continued, "They got one doctor here in Kiowa, but he's been busy day and night. There are other doctors in line waiting to register, but they don't want to lose their place and they won't come to our camp. We may have to take him along the line, ask for a doctor, but it's so awful out there—" She shook her head and fell silent.

"How is it bad out at the line?" Her worry climbed. Her Ad was there, staying in place to make the Run.

"The heat's even worse out there, than here where we got a few trees. The temperature is above a hundred most every day, then nights it gets awful cold. Some of the folks have been in line for days with little to eat or drink, just breathing thick dust. One or two already dropped dead where they stood—"

"They *died* in line?" It seemed impossible, and yet, given the conditions, she supposed that could be true.

The woman went on, "Others took sick with sunstroke are barely hanging on. There's arguments, fighting, knifings and shootings. Everybody knows there's not going to be land enough to go around, but each one believes he will be one of the lucky ones. Every man out there is wearing a gun. It's worse than a war, seems to me. And just about as bad here in town, truth to tell."

"Will you stay?" Lucy Ann asked. "Do you think your man can get well, here?"

The woman shook her head. "I honestly don't know. We came hoping to make a new life in the Strip. But now that my man's took sick, I just don't know. Well, I do know what he would want. He would want son and me to go ahead and make the Run. But I wish we had stayed to home in Medicine Lodge and never come." She nodded at her son, on the other side of her wobbly husband, that she was ready to go back to their camp. "If Elgin wasn't so sick and could hear me say that, it would make him plumb mad."

They stumbled away in the pale morning light, the man's toes leaving twin trails in the dust between them. The tall woman said over her shoulder, "We are the Lortons from Medicine Lodge. Good luck to you and your family, Missus."

She called after them, "We're the Walsh family from Paragon Springs, we're Lucy Ann, Admire, and Rachel. Good luck to you, too, Lortons."

While Rachel gave their horses a ration of water and grain, Lucy Ann couldn't move quickly enough to prepare breakfast for Ad. The bacon had hardly cooled from the skillet before she wrapped it in cloth with cornbread left-over from last night's supper. She filled a small covered bucket with stew she had simmered late last night, filled a second tin pail with hot coffee, clamped on the lid and put the stew and coffee with his breakfast in a tote sack.

She tied on her yellow sunbonnet that matched her faded yellow muslin dress, strapped a canteen of the pre-cious water over her shoulder, ate a few bites herself, and she was ready to go.

Rachel elected to stay at camp to see that nothing was stolen. Lucy Ann hesitated, not wanting to leave her there alone. She had been thinking earlier to dismantle their tent and take all their belongings and both of them drive out to find Ad—if they could get the wagon out of camp, it was so crowded. She had given up the plan chiefly because finding a second campsite, later, would be impossible. She gave Ra-chel the gun. "Don't let anybody come near."

She threaded her way on foot through groups of people, camps of ragged tents. She circled weathered wagons and tethered animals, stepped carefully over piles of dung. Flies droned everywhere. The hot morning air was rife with the stench of animal offal, unwashed humans, and unbelievable odors from primitive toilet facilities. Always a very clean person, she found it hard not to gag and give up her breakfast.

She noted sympathetically that most of the horses and mules, and most of their owners, looked gaunt from hunger and thirst. She realized that many must have arrived in that condition, having suffered the drought and depression where they came from. Almost every man, regardless of his past life as merchant, cowboy, farmer, or other profession, wore a gun, as Mrs. Lorton said. To a man they looked like they wouldn't take kindly to being crossed, either. They all wanted land, but some of them, as sure as the sun came up in the east and set west, were not going to succeed.

She neared the registration booths, a series of dusty tents being manned by bustling, sweating clerks in high-collar suits.

The waiting line, four and five people abreast, stretched wavering as far eastward as her eye could follow. Mostly they were men, but there were women, too, some of them held parasols against the punishing sun.

She studied the tired dirty faces of hundreds of strangers, looking for Ad. She sought some sign of his paint horse. There were several Indian, or Chickasaw ponies among the bays, sorrels, grays, roans, and blacks tethered near their owners so they would have special care, and not be stolen. Most of the horses were farm animals or smaller mustang cow-ponies. Some of the rest looked to be fast, thoroughbred racehorses. A sleek coal-black gelding particularly caught her eye. There was a chance that Admire's fast pony would not be fast enough in the scramble for claims.

As Lucy Ann walked on, beneath her dress perspiration ran in rivulets down her back, pooled under her breasts and at the top of her waistline. So far, she hadn't spotted Admire. There had to be thousands in the line before him, just like he said. Eventually, she saw a familiar-looking face under a tipped-back hat. The man squatted in line with three or four other fellows, drifter-types by their appearance, and they were shooting dice in the dirt. She walked over to them. "Mr. Thorne? Aren't you Harlan Thorne, my friend Aurelia's brother-in-law?"

He looked up, surprised, but he grinned. His own dark brow was beaded with perspiration as he tipped his hat to her, showing a thatch of salt and pepper hair. He looked at her from merry blue eyes as he repeated, "Am I the brother-in-law of Paragon Springs's lady mayor? I reckon I am, although Aurelia don't like claimin' me."

She half-smiled. "I'm looking for my husband, Admire Walsh. He rides an Indian pony. You may remember him from our auction; you came to our farm sale with Aurelia's family when we sold out back in Paragon Springs. Have you seen Ad?"

It was a foolish question, considering the thousands of people in the vast camp-settlement. But Harlan nodded as he stood up to face her. "Saw him once to say howdy, he was headin' back to get in line." He motioned with his head to the ribbon of people stretching east. "He's back there, somewhere. I think he met up with some friends. Some of them was fellows I remember meetin' at your sale, Mrs. Walsh."

"Thank you very much." She felt guilty, almost wanted to hide the tote sack of food. It fretted her to think that others might guess what it contained. In any other instance she would offer to share with folks who looked to be hungry and thirsty. But there were *thousands* in the line and there was no way she could feed even a few of them. She had barely enough victuals for Admire. He was her first concern, even though she would have liked to feed them all.

Harlan Thorne seemed to answer her thoughts as he said, confidently, "This waitin' in line ain't goin' to last forever, we'll all get rich and fat once we stake our claims in Oklahoma."

She gave him a relieved smile, and decided that if she could find some flour so that she might bake extra batches of bread in her Dutch Oven, it might help to relieve the hunger for some. She would look into it, although her guess was that if water was in short supply in Kiowa, flour and other staples would be also, due to the hordes that had descended.

She had walked only a short way after telling Thorne goodbye, when a rough-looking man in line called out to her, "Say, lady in yellow, come on over here. Share your grub and water with me, sweet gal, and I'll share my claim with you, rest'a my life."

"I can't, sorry." She shook her head, hid a smile, and walked a little faster. A sidewise glance showed him laughing and doffing his hat to her. His hat had so many holes in it she guessed that it had been used for target practice to kill time in the line.

Farther on, she spotted a familiar, beloved, dust-coated hat and black beard among the many. In spite of the heat, she ran. "Ad, oh, Admire, I thought I'd never find you."

"Lucy Ann, you're a sight for sore eyes!" He welcomed her with hands outstretched, a light in his eyes. He looked tired, she thought; every inch of him was coated with dust. His Indian pony was tethered nearby in a patch of dead grass mostly eaten away. But he had a bucket with grain in the bottom, that he'd been feeding his horse, and a bale of hay he must have bought from someone. He frowned, then. "Are you all right? Where is Rachel, is she all right?"

Men in line near him stepped back a pace or two to give them a shred of privacy.

"We're both fine. I left her at our camp to make sure nothing gets stolen." She had already decided not to mention the sick man who had broken into their tent and got into bed with her. He would realize, as she did, that it could happen again and the next fellow might not be innocent. Nor did she want to tell him that she had had to pay cash for their water.

But he asked, as she handed him the canteen, "D'ya have to pay for this?"

She nodded. "There's little water to be had, Admire. Townsfolk either refuse to let you have water from their well, or they charge dear for it. I'm sorry, Ad, I know it seems a foolish way to use our money, but there is no other choice. The river is dry, Rachel and I went to look." And yet, water was needed for them and their stock to stay alive and well.

He nodded, then leaned forward to whisper close to her ear, "You might follow the river back quite a ways, Lucy Ann, you or Rachel, and maybe you'll find a little water in a deep hole. Lofty Gowdy located some water upstream, he and Bama and me have been taking turns toting water for our horses."

"We'll go looking. If I boil the water, it may be all right to drink and to cook with. We certainly need it for our horses."

He explained that some church folks from town had come out to the line with sandwiches to sell to those who could afford them. They were selling sunbonnets to the

27

women in line, too. "They was selling water for ten cents a cup. Another bunch was selling water for a dollar a pint. I decided to wait for you." He took a long draught from the canteen, wolfed at the cornbread and bacon she gave him.

She told him that she had looked for his friends along the way, but hadn't spotted them. The only person she had recognized the whole distance was Harlan Thorne. "Where are all the men you mean to stake claims with?"

"They're right here close. Lofty Gowdy and a half dozen of the boys is up there about twenty yards." He stretched to try and see them over the heads in the line and stroked his beard. "Bama ain't far ahead of them. Flan is somewhere back of me."

She looked ahead to where he pointed and recognized a few of his friends. At home they were ordinary, clean-dressed middle-aged cowboys, like Admire. Here they were covered with filth and sported full beards and it was no wonder she hadn't spotted them. Bama was so coated with gray dust you couldn't tell he was a black man. "I see them now," she said, and smiled.

She told him the gossip she had overheard about the use of trains in the Run. "They claim the trains will be held back slow so that they won't outrun the wagons and horses to the best claims."

"I heard that, too. I hope it's true they keep them trains at fifteen miles an hour. I know my pony can outrun the wagons and most of the horses, but I'd rather not have to race a train at full bore. I mean to make my claim, but I don't intend to kill my horse doin' it."

She brought up the subject of Sooners, people hid out in the Strip waiting to grab the best claims.

He nodded. "I don't doubt there are plenty of them in there. They've known for a month the Run was going to happen. Some folks were sent in legal, to dig wells at each planned townsite so there will be water aplenty for the new settlers when they get there. There's land agents in there already, prepared to file our claims once we stake them. There's sheriffs and probate judges on hand to take on their duties soon's we get there. But the unlawful Sooners got something to worry about. Soldiers, cavalry troops from Fort Reno, Fort Supply and Fort Riley are already in the Strip, ordered to clear out everybody that's not supposed to be there. If they don't roust out willingly, the soldiers have orders to flush them out by setting fires."

"They'll burn them out? But somebody could be bad hurt, or burned to death!"

"Maybe they won't set fires, if them Sooners do as they're told. I hope they don't need to burn 'em out, it's hot as Hades without set fires to add to the misery." He mopped his forehead with his sleeve. "Could get dangerous, the whole country burn up. I don't expect them Sooners to move peaceable, but I sure hope they do."

"Yes, so do I." She considered a moment, then asked, although she was already sure what his reply would be, "Couldn't Rachel and I take turns with you waiting here in line? One of us could hold your place, and you could go back and get some rest in our tent—"

He looked at her, almost angry, "I don't want neither of you out in this here line! It's not safe. I know it's not exactly paradise where you are, but it's worse out here. There's gamblin', cheatin', arguments. I wish I had a dime for every gun that's gone off reckless."

She nodded, although she thought there might be some doubt about their camp close to town being any safer. But she also knew he didn't trust anyone but himself to hold his place in line and he could be very stubborn.

"Got real cold last night, didn't it?" he changed the subject. "Funny, it can be real scorchin' in the daytime, people gettin' sick and droppin' from the heat. I heard that another fellow, from New Jersey I think they said, died today. At night, the temperature drops and you can practically hear people shivering and their teeth clacking from the cold."

"Can I bring you an extra blanket?" she asked anxiously.

"No, no, I don't need no extra blanket. I stay awake most nights, anyhow, sittin' up wrapped in the one I got. Got to make sure nobody steals my horse." His voice softened, "It's just nice to have you come out here, bring me food and water and visit me, Lucy Ann. I want you to know that, how much I appreciate you."

"I know you do, Ad." She stood on tiptoe and kissed his cheek. He glanced self-consciously at the other men around them, held her against him for a slight second, then let her go. She told him, "I need to get back to our camp, I don't like leaving Rachel alone, but I'll see you again tomorrow."

He nodded, and motioned for her to go.

On the way back to camp, she stopped to visit with tall, stringbean-thin, Lofty Gowdy, and a couple of Ad's other friends. They wore white-toothed grins and bright eyes in their dusty faces and were as hopeful and determined as Admire, and she began to believe that they might succeed, the wonderful dream of their own shared ranch just might happen.

September 16th, only a few days away now, held the answer one way or the other.

If Ad and his friends all survived it, this Run might be looked back on as the greatest event in their lives—as well as the most trying.

Chapter Three

For the next two days, Lucy Ann and Rachel took turns watering the horses from the stagnant pool in the river upstream and taking food and water to Ad at the line. The temperature ranged at 110 degrees each day; dust blew in the hot winds, as well as ash from the fires the soldiers had set to drive out the Sooners.

Lines grew longer and longer at the town wells. The level of water in the wells sank, and though it was brackish and scummy, it got more expensive.

Of the many thousands waiting to register and make the Run, many collapsed, some died, but no one gave up to go back home. Every soul there thought they would be lucky and get a fine claim in the promised land of the Cherokee Strip. Suffering seemed to mean nothing, although the lines for registration were being referred to as "Lines Of Death" in the newspapers.

Tensions climbed as the day and hour for the race neared. Lucy Ann heard one man say that he would shoot to kill to get a claim, if it came to that. She told Admire about it, he admitted he had heard the same from other men, and he was prepared. He would take his claim legal, but he would get a claim and he would keep it.

Lucy Ann was deeply worried for him, but she felt a toll being taken on herself as well. Her head had begun to pain her almost constantly. It worried her that she had to make an unheard of number of trips to the hastily constructed outhouse at the edge of their camp. She decided that unpleasantness was due to drinking bad water; she would get over it.

She felt unusually weak, her nights were spent restlessly tossing; just tending her chores by day took all of her strength. Her abdomen hurt like fire and had nothing to do with her monthlies.

It was the pressing heat day after day that was responsible, she reminded herself, when her appetite left her. Who could feel well when there was not enough clean water to drink, or any water to use to take a proper bath? Everyone was suffering. Thorne was right when he said these miseries wouldn't last forever, but they couldn't end any too soon for her.

She was glad to see Friday, the fifteenth of September, arrive. Next day at noon the starting guns would be fired and the grand race for the last free lands would be on.

In those last hours, like a gigantic circus, the mass encampment stirred, erratically and with mean determination. Wagons rolled out of the camp to take their place in line for the race. Horses were given special treatment. Tall bicycles ridden by derby-hatted dandies, small carts driven by women, and hundreds of riders on horseback joined the melee to take their place in line to wait out the night and the next morning.

Lucy Ann knew the picture was the same along the entire 276-mile Strip. Rumor had it that between 100,000 and 150,000 would be making the Run, thousands more, like herself, would be standing by to witness it.

In a near-stupor, Lucy Ann watched their camp and the town thin out and was glad. With so many making the Run and spending the night in the Strip on their new claims, maybe she and Rachel had a chance for a hotel room, or a room in one of the two boarding houses for the rest of their stay. She wanted to be well when Ad came to get them for the trip to their new claim. She was sure that just a few hours or days under more civilized conditions would take care of her miseries.

When she tried to get out of bed the morning of the sixteenth her muscles felt like oatmeal and wouldn't cooperate. Her skull felt split with pain and it was hard to focus her eyes. In dragging motions she managed to dress in her old red calico, wash her face, and tend to her hair somewhat.

Rachel was already up, preparing breakfast outside. Lucy Ann stood in the doorway of the tent, gripping the flaps, trying to find the strength to stay on her feet and keep moving. She went out to their fire on feeble, vibrating legs, and sat down quickly on a feed box.

"Good grief, Mama! Are you all right?" Rachel asked, her face filled with worry.

She waved Rachel off with a shaking hand. "Y-yes, I'm fine. Just a little tired. The heat, the dust, bothers me, I suppose. But I'm really all right."

"Are you sure, Mama? You don't look well at all." She jumped up and hastened to feel Lucy Ann's forehead. "You have a fever—! Your nose is starting to bleed." She ran and brought her mother a cloth for her nose.

"It's the heat." She was panting as she took the cloth and put it to her nose, then gently brushed Rachel's hands away. "Don't fuss, Rachel. And whatever you do, don't say anything about this to your papa, not today. I'm going to be all right. Once the race is over, we'll get a room at the hotel." She managed a small, dry chuckle. "Maybe I'll stay in bed a day or two."

Rachel shook her head. "I don't know if I should listen to you, Mama. You look truly sick to me. You are flushed, your eyes don't look right; now this nosebleed. Maybe we should find a room for you right now—?"

"No!" her answer was vehement. "I will be at the race to see your father off. That is that. A little touch of the heat and the miseries of this place are all that's wrong, I'm telling you."

She tried to eat, but her tongue was a thick furry log in her mouth and it was impossible. She pretended that the excitement of the big day robbed her appetite when she set the plate aside. Rachel didn't appear convinced, and didn't particularly respond. But she eyed Lucy Ann worriedly every little bit.

They believed it safe to leave their belongings unguarded with the camp virtually cleared out. They could both go to watch the race. Rachel took Lucy Ann's arm to steady her on the long walk.

At the line Lucy Ann forced her whole attention on Ad and the momentous event he was about to be involved in. She knew that she would never again see so many people—men, women, and children of all ages—in one place with a single goal in mind: land, a new home, a new life.

Just at sundown yesterday, Ad had reached the registration booth. He had his certificate to make the Run, his stake and flag. The booths had stayed open all night, would issue certificates up to the hour of the race. Anyone without a certificate at that time would be out of luck, although the clerks vowed they would register everyone in time.

Suspense was as thick as was the dust under the blazing sun. As noon neared, soldiers rode up and down the lines maintaining order. The swaying black line stretched as far as the eye could see and contained every variety of conveyance with people aboard: covered wagons, buggies, bicycles, and pony carts. Riders had at the ready their draft horses, cow-ponies, and thoroughbred racehorses they would ride. There were humans on foot, prepared to run, with their few worldly possessions in a pack on their back, a stick in hand to ward off snakes and competition.

In those last moments, Lucy Ann kissed Ad. Women didn't do that sort of thing in public, but it felt important to kiss him for good luck. He had eaten the breakfast they brought him that morning mechanically, his mind preoccupied. For likely the thousandth time he had studied the map he and his friends had made for the area they meant to claim.

He had had little to say until now, when he told her, studying her face, "You look awful red from the sun, Lucy Ann; get on out of it as soon as you can. Take care of yourself, til I come for you and Rachel. That may be a week, or maybe it'll be a month. The rules say that after I find my claim and drive my stake—and it'll be best if I got a witness—I can go personally to the land office to file. The law says that's got to be done in a reasonable time, but there could be a long wait at the land office."

She nodded that she understood and managed a smile.

"You got provisions to last?" he wanted to know, and she nodded. The truth was, they had brought a large share of their food supply for Ad to take with him for his first days out at the new claim. She was sure she and Rachel could manage in the town somehow.

"Bout ready," Ad swung up onto his horse. He said over his shoulder, "You two stand back so's you don't get hurt."

Rachel caught her when her steps proved unsteady. Lucy Ann moved free, stood straight. "Good luck, Admire." He waved a hand that he heard and thanked her.

Examination showed that up and down the line Admire's friends were ready to make the ride. They waved at Ad and he waved at them.

"I wonder where the Lortons are?" Lucy Ann said, trying to spot them.

"They might've returned home and aren't making the run; the father was very ill," Rachel commented and Lucy Ann nodded.

Soldiers with carbine rifles were stationed every 600 yards waiting to fire the signal-shot at exactly noon. They also had orders to fire at anyone who broke the line ahead of time.

Minutes, seconds, ticked by. There were excited murmurs all up and down the line, and soft, confident exclamations. Then, at high noon, rifle-fire exploded and the race was on with a thunder of noise and yelling.

Leading the rush were the men and women on horseback; light carts were close behind, then came buckboards, spring wagons, buggies, and heavy farm wagons. Mixed in the dusty flying melee were men on bicycles and on foot. Lucy Ann saw the Lortons, then, the sick man wrapped up in the back of the wagon, Mrs. Lorton driving, their son beside her. Lucy Ann mentally wished them good fortune.

Within two minutes, Ad, Lofty Gowdy, Bama, and most of his other friends, were out of sight. The wagons and buggies grew smaller and smaller in the simmering, dusty, blue-white distance. The thick dust of the ground behind them was littered with feed boxes, buckets, and bales of hay that had bounced out of vehicles in the rush. A woman, bounced out of the back of a cart driven by a younger woman, picked herself up and began to follow on foot.

There was a stillness, then, as though there wasn't life enough left for movement, or sound.

Lucy Ann stood for a while longer, unexplainable tears in her eyes as she watched the spot where Ad had disappeared. Then she turned, weaving on her feet, to Rachel,

"Now, honey, give me a hand so we can get out of this place."

Slowly, they made their way back to the village. The town was nearly deserted. Rubble was everywhere. Abandoned campfires still smoldered. The actual town, the streets, could be seen clearly for the first time. A store, a saloon, a lawyer's office, a feedstore, stood out. It was not a bad looking town, in some ways it reminded Lucy Ann of Paragon Springs.

Some homes were built of sod and others were frame houses; quite a few of them appeared empty, their owners likely taking part in the Run.

She noted dimly that some structures, business-houses, were already being taken apart, to be hauled to new towns in the Strip and reassembled.

"Find us a room, a real room with a bed, if you can find a hotel or boarding place still standing and operating," she admonished Rachel through a dry throat. The dry dusty world in the white-hot sunshine was beginning to swim and in another minute it might vanish altogether. Just as Admire had disappeared into oblivion, in that cloud of dust.

Chapter Four

Lucy Ann swam in and out of consciousness for days, sometimes seeing a room with rose-colored wallpaper through her aching, sun-seared eyes. In a few of those half-conscious times, she believed she lay in that room in a real bed. There was another presence with her, Ad, or Rachel. But when a voice told her to "lie quietly if she wanted to get well, to live," it was a stranger's.

Sometimes she tasted oil of turpentine and her tongue didn't seem so dry; after, she could swallow, breathe a little easier.

Cool fingers would hold the inside of her wrist or feel her brow, stirring her for a few seconds out of the dimness, the dark clouds that seemed to hold her within them.

She was aware sometimes, of being forced to lie back, other times lifted to swallow a chalky liquid. "The medicine, morphine sulphate, bismuth, and creosote, is for her diarrhea," the strange voice explained to someone. And when she tried to get up, "The laudanum will settle her restlessness. She must remain very still as exertion can be fatal."

Then one morning she came gradually out of the darkness to find Rachel giving her a cool sponge bath. She moved her hand shakily to cover her daughter's. "R-Rachel." It was hard to speak, her throat was dry, her tongue uncooperative, but she managed to whisper, "Where is Admire? Did your papa get back to town yet? Has he come for us?"

Rachel gave her a teary, exceptionally happy smile. "You're awake!" When she saw that Lucy Ann was trying to speak again she told her, "Papa hasn't come back from the Strip, Mama, but it's too soon. I'm sure he's all right. He just has lots to do before he's ready for us."

"How—long since the d-day of the Run? How long have I been here? Where—?"

"Papa's been gone a week. You nearly died, Mama," Rachel answered solemnly, "but the doctor says you've turned a corner and will surely mend, with care." She wiped at a tear. "You have a very serious typhoid fever-like disease and you've a long recovery ahead of you."

"Where—are we?" Lucy Ann asked again.

Rachel nodded, put a finger to her lips for Lucy Ann to be still. "We're in a room at the doctor's house here in Kiowa, we've been here since the day of the Run—"

"We can't afford a doc—" Lucy Ann began before Rachel's cool palm settled gently over her mouth.

"Shh, Mama. I'm paying for our keep by nursing other patients as well as you. There were folks bad hurt the day of the Run. One man was thrown from his horse, he has a fractured skull and a broken arm. Another man was brought here badly burned. He was caught in a fire set by a Sooner to keep legal homesteaders off the claim he meant to have. Others seem to have the same sickness you have, although there doesn't seem to be a name for it. The doctor feels it was brought on by the drought conditions, poor drinking water, and folks' own general poor health in these hard times. He had to send to Wichita for a new shipment of medicines. He'd used up all he had while folks were here for the Run."

Lucy Ann nodded, her eyes blinked drowsily of their own accord. Then, Rachel retrieved a cup of beef tea from the bedside table and, slipping her hand under Lucy Ann's head, urged her to take at least a few sips. "Beef tea and some barley water are all you can have for now, Mama. Doctor says later you can have an egg in milk, or meat soup to make you strong."

Again Lucy Ann nodded, and took as much of the beef tea as she could. She licked her dry cracked lips. She wanted to be strong when Admire came. She could not let him see her like this, flat on her back in bed. She had always been sturdy, as a girl and later as a woman. She'd had very few sick days in her life, and she didn't mean to give in to such now.

She was feeling proud of herself, had lain back drowsily, when her stomach roiled and churned against the tea and then brought it up in an explosive gush. Rachel, in one quick motion, swept a porcelain bowl under her chin to catch the mess.

Later, Rachel washed her face and her mouth. The cool wetness felt good, although it set her to shivering uncontrollably.

"You're still running a temperature, Mama, but you have begun to get better. You must lie very still, rest and sleep, until you're able to be up again."

Lucy Ann, feeling too ill at the moment to reply, closed her eyes. Rachel's cool kiss met her cheek. "That's right, go to sleep, Mama. I'll check on you again soon." She rustled out of the room with steps that seemed confident and happy.

A few days later, Lucy Ann was more fully awake and feeling some better when she was visited by the tall doctor, who introduced himself as Doctor Olaf Jensen.

"I'm better," she told him in a weak voice, but as strong as she could make it, before he could tell her otherwise.

"Yes, you are," he agreed with a chuckle, his fingers

clasped the inside of her wrist. "Your pulse is falling off in frequency, it's almost back to normal." He released her wrist, touched her forehead with the back of his hand. "Your temperature is somewhat diminished but you're still dehydrated. You need to drink more liquid—water and beef tea. In a day or two we might try some milk thickened with tapioca, and see if you can keep that down."

"Real food would make me strong," she ventured huskily. She tried to lift her head from the pillow but it was like a hundred-pound stone that wouldn't budge. She lay quivering, taking slow deep breaths. How could simply trying to take her head from the pillow wear her down so, make her feel so weak?

The doctor was shaking his head. "You can't have real food, not yet. Your stomach and bowels couldn't handle solid foods. No fruits at all, either. But I think you're almost ready for an egg beaten up with milk, and some milk thickened with tapioca; they will serve you fine for a time. And please," he added, "keep drinking beef tea, lots of it."

She was silent for a moment, then told him, "I want to thank you, Dr. Jensen. My daughter, Rachel, tells me you saved my life."

"Some haven't been so lucky," he admitted.

Her throat constricted and she felt very sad, knowing he spoke about Mr. Lorton. Rachel had told her that the Lortons had failed to find a claim and had returned to Kiowa. Elgin Lorton lived only a day after their return. After his burial in the Kiowa cemetery, Mrs. Lorton and their son had returned to Medicine Lodge.

Doctor Jensen phrased his next remark as a question, his blond eyebrows quirked in study, "Maybe you have a strong constitution and that's bringing you through as much as my treatment?"

"I'm beholden for your care, for letting me and my daughter stay here—"

He shook his head, said sincerely, "Your bill is paid in full by your daughter. I don't know what I would have done without her help the past week and a half. The insanity of the Run—well, it's over." He started for the door, then turned, "Rachel tells me your husband will be coming for you to take you down to his new claim in the Strip? I hope it won't be too soon, you won't be ready to travel for some time yet."

She wanted help in sitting up, wanted to dangle her legs over the side of the bed and try to regain some of her energy. But both Rachel and Dr. Jensen argued her down. He insisted that she must not sit up in bed until she had spent several days fever-free.

He cautioned her continually that exertion could cause a relapse.

As the days passed, she felt helpless, restless, imprisoned by the bed. But at the same time, she wanted to follow orders, to recover and be especially strong and able when Ad came for them. She would drown herself in beef tea if that's what it took.

And then came the day when Rachel entered her room with tears flooding her eyes; her face was white with shock, the expression in her eyes was disbelieving. "We have company, Mama," she whispered. She stood aside and Ad's friends, Lofty Gowdy and copper-haired Flan Jones, ambled into the room, hats held down at their waists, distress altering their features.

"What is it?" Dread gripped Lucy Ann.

Rachel came over to kneel by her bed; she put her forehead on Lucy Ann's hand where it lay trembling on the sheet. "It's Papa," she whispered, "it's Papa."

In those first few moments she felt that if she rejected what these friends of Ad were about to tell her, then that would make it untrue. She ignored the cold sensation in the pit of her stomach. She lay quiet, stoic, while Lofty and Flan told her a terrible, terrible lie that she knew down deep was the truth. And what she had feared from the first.

"Admire made a good ride," Lofty said, stroking his long jaw. "He really did. He got to the claim he wanted, legal, and drove his stake." His eyes were shiny with a mixture of sympathy and anger. "There was a fella', a worthless no-good, maybe a tenth of a mile behind him. He got to the claim, shot Admire, pulled his stake, and drove his own. There are witnesses, but the man who killed Admire says his statement is the truth; that he was there first and was only defending himself and the claim. The law is looking into it."

Flan Jones took over. "The rest of us all got claims, like we planned with Ad, a half-mile apart so we'd have one big spread. Admire didn't—didn't die right off. We thought he'd get better, that when he got back on his feet we'd be able to take him to the land office and make his claim legal with the agent." Words seemed to lodge in his throat, and then he told her, "Ad died three days ago, we had to bury him there where we was. We come to tell you as soon as we could."

Lofty spoke again, moving a few steps closer to Lucy Ann, and turning his hat round and round in his long brown fingers. "Until the courts settle who the claim belongs to, officially, we want you and Rachel to come down there and share our place, share it with us even if the court finds in that murdering skunk's favor. Ad made the ride, and you've got comin' all we can provide you, just as he would've done. We come to take you with us.'"

Tears were running down the sides of Lucy Ann's face, dampening her hair; she stroked the back of Rachel's head. She spoke past her pain, "We thank you boys, truly. But Admire isn't there on the claim, and I don't think we want to be there, either, not without him. I believe we will go home, to Paragon Springs."

Rachel raised her head, her face was blotched and swollen from crying, but even in her grave sadness she looked hopeful.

"But, Lucy Ann," Flan protested, running his hand through his copper hair, "Admire's claim is now lawfully yours, as his widow. The land courts are likely to decide that, decide in Ad's favor, your favor."

"When might that be, when would Ad's case go to court?"

Both men shook their heads. Lofty admitted, "Could happen in a few months, or it could take years, they's going to be hundreds of contested claims."

"I wouldn't want to wait that long to learn what might happen," she told them simply.

Lofty growled, a frown stamped on his leathery brown face, "There were too many folks in the Run for the amount of land available. The government's plan didn't work out the way they expected. Problem was, three to six settlers would swarm to *different areas* in a single quarter section, each one of 'em claiming to be first. Sometimes they was ten claimants to a quarter section, an' that only caused gunplay, an' somebody endin' up dead like in Ad's case. Once in a while a claimant settled the argument by selling out to the others, for one hundred dollars to three hundred dollars. Quite a few just packed up and left the country without a whimper."

Ad stood up for his rights and was killed for doing so.

"We have Admire's pinto for you," Flan was saying. "He's a damn good horse."

"I don't want him."

Rachel looked sharply at her. Lucy Ann continued, "I want you men to have him, keep him down there in the Strip and work him on your ranch. That's what Ad wanted. And you can have the use of Ad's claim," she added, "if the land-office officials decide in the end that he was first." Her voice caught, "But Rachel and I are going home."

It took Lofty and Flan a long time to be convinced, but they agreed to look out for her affairs when Admire's case came up. They knew the witnesses, they knew everybody involved. They had met some of the land agents in their region and they thought they would be fair. They would keep her informed.

"How you going to get back to Paragon Springs?" Lofty asked, leaning toward her with concern darkening his blue eyes. "You two can't make that trip alone and with you still sick, Lucy Ann."

We will get there any way we can, she wanted to say but Flan had come up with another idea.

"Listen," he said, "I think you know a fella' by the name of Harlan Thorne? I heard him talkin' the other day when he was over to the land office the same time we was. He said he's going back to Paragon Springs real soon! He's goin' there after a friend of his, an old fella' named Knob, so's he can bring him down to the Strip to share his claim. He should be passing through Kiowa in about a week on his way up to Hodgeman County. It'd be best if you ladies let him see you there all right, if you won't change your mind and come down to Oklahoma with us."

"Can you get word to Mr. Thorne?" Both men nodded.

"Then tell him we would take it kindly if he would let us travel with him to Paragon Springs. Tell him where to find us. We'll be ready."

The news of Ad's death, the talk of what she and Rachel must do now, had sapped Lucy Ann of the strength she'd gained in the last few days. She lay limp and listless, giving into hard sobs after his friends left, crying until she was drained. "I knew," she whispered to Rachel, "I knew something like this might happen. I was so afraid—"

Rachel clasped her hands. "But you stood by Papa, even so, Mama. You always did whatever he wanted. He was good to us, but you returned that to him, full-score. You would have given him the moon if you could have—"

"Yes," she said, lifting her hand to their daughter's tear-wet cheek, "I would have given him the moon."

But now we're going back home, to pick up the pieces of our broken life and somehow go on.

One good thing, Rachel would soon be with her David.

She wished she knew how she could live the remainder of her life without Admire.

Chapter Five

Seventeen Years Later

Paragon Springs, April, 1910. Lucy Ann's clean clothes popped in the hot wind, filling her face as she tried to unpin them from the clothesline. "Drat!" Pushing them away, she continued to take down and fold them into the basket at her feet. Catching sight over the rope line of her neighbor's place to the northwest, she frowned in annoyance.

Where old Mr. Eben Reilly used to grow corn, Russian thistles flourished and were crackling dry in the hot sun. Half the fence lines around the farm needed fixing and the house and outbuildings begged for fresh paint. How could Tom Reilly, a full-grown able-bodied man, be so neglectful of a perfectly good farm? And who was he, anyway, so strange?

She knew him only by sight, a tall, fortyish man in city-duds, they'd traded little talk. He had moved in last winter, taking over the place his grandfather left to him when he had died a year and a half ago.

Maybe, if Tom Reilly had had to work hard for his farm, the way most people around Paragon Springs had had to do, instead of inheriting it, he would take better care of the place.

Her own farm, not a large one, just eighty acres, was laid out like a tidy quilt. In good seasons it was pretty as a picture. She enjoyed keeping a fresh coat of paint on her buildings, the fences mended, the weeds out as best she could. Any harness or equipment repair she couldn't do herself she turned over the minute it was needed to the newest Paragon Springs blacksmith, Frank Pickering.

In the east pasture, her milk cow and a half-dozen sheep grazed. Her four horses fed in another pasture, southward. In a neat pen she had built next to the barn were her two rooting pigs and the sow's piglets. She kept them fat with kitchen scraps, corncobs, and cow's milk. A small sod henhouse under a cottonwood tree in the side-yard housed her dozen Rhode Island Red hens and rooster at night, by day they were let out to roam for grasshoppers and other insects.

Her kitchen garden was laid off in perfect rows just off her back porch near the well. Beyond the farmstead proper she had planted a few acres of broomcorn, a good cash crop for the making of brooms, and some winter wheat. This spring she worried about her crops. In a season when farmers especially needed rain, three months had passed without a drop of moisture. She carried water from the well to her garden by the bucketful which was very tiring on a woman. The newly sprouted broomcorn and wheat would likely scorch and die if they didn't get rain, soon.

Maybe it was the vagaries of western Kansas weather that kept Tom Reilly from trying to wrest a competence from his farm? Although it wasn't her business, she would like to know.

Anyhow, it was a disgrace to see, in her opinion. If Mr. Reilly was simply lazy he ought to get rid of the farm, sell it to someone who would appreciate it. As she looked again in that direction, a fluorescent zig-zag of lightning rent the hazy sky further to the north. Her mood suddenly switched, her spirits rising. *Rain?* The lightning was miles away toward Ness City, but still it could mean rain, rain that would eventually fall over her farm.

She finished gathering her laundry, looked again to see if the storm was building. It wasn't. Instead, this time, clouds of silvery smoke swirled and spread fast at ground level. Prairie fire set by the lightning! And every blade of grass between there and where she stood, open country, was tinder dry. Her panic climbed. Water was scarce since they had had no recent rains to replenish the creeks and wells.

As she raced toward the house with her clothes-basket on her hip she recalled the story of a woman who poured milk on her house to try and save it from fire. Years back, that had happened. She couldn't remember if the fire was put out. She hoped she wouldn't be faced with such drastic measures.

Inside her small white frame cottage, she frantically tried to think what was most important to save if the fire spread that far. She wanted all of her few treasures, but decided she would be best off saving the little tin box on the high shelf of her wardrobe. She hurried to the bedroom and took the box down, then wondered what to do with it. She couldn't carry it on her person fighting fire.

Her little dog, only last month before he was bitten by a rattlesnake and died, had dug a two-foot deep hole behind the henhouse. His grave was on a knoll in the pasture. She hadn't yet filled in the hole he had dug. She ran there, placed the tin box at the bottom of the hole, quickly piled dirt over it and tamped it down tight. She felt a trifle better then and her glance zipped about for the next chore. She ran for the barnyard.

Her chickens already ran loose. She freed the pigs from their pen so they could reach the creek if they had to. She gathered enough panicked breath to whistle in her golden bay riding horse, Taffy, from the pasture, led her to the barn and quickly saddled up. Tapping Taffy's sides with the

reins, she raced through the pasture, leaning down to open
gates so her other horses and milk cow could flee the fire if
it came that far, and then swung back toward the barn.

Over her shoulder she saw that the smoke clouds were
traveling fast, she could smell the fire on the wind. The
heat-hazy sky resembled a rosy sunset. At the barn, she
bundled feed sacks and a horse blanket and tied it behind
the cantle of her saddle. Then she was on her way in a hard
lope toward her neighbor's farm.

His place was in line of the blaze before hers. She'd warn
him, then ride on to fight the fire. She galloped through
open fields of stirrup-high thistles that made her nearly sick
to see. What kind of feed was that for his milk cow, his
horse? No one answered her knock on the back door of her
house. She climbed back on Taffy and rode to the barn
where she again dismounted. She flung open the barn door.

Lucy Ann was startled to see that he had gutted the
barn, and he was working with a soldering tool shoulder-
height on a large web of metal pipes or rods. The contraption looked like an enormous dragon-fly or the skeleton of a
turkey vulture with two sets of wings, one on top of the
other. Jolted back to reality she shouted at him, "Mr. Reilly!
Prairie fire, coming this way. Free your stock, you need to
look after your house—!"

His blue eyes looked at her blankly for a moment and his
fingers plowed a furrow through his thick silvery hair before
he absorbed what she was telling him. His lean form made a
couple of wild leaps and turns. Horror filled his face, his
dark brown brows arched, "Fire? Not here, not my *barn!*
Not all my hard work—" he motioned at the web of rods,
"destroyed!" He lunged toward the dusty, cob-webby barn
window, looked out, turned back to her. "The fire seems to
be quite far away. We have to stop it before it gets here.

What can we do? Is there a fire crew to help us?"

She mustered patience with the greenhorn. "The fire is miles away but it will travel fast. Others have seen it by now, probably. The first thing *you* need to do is see to your animals, your house." *Forget the silly whatchamacallit!*

"I have to find something to cover—" he stammered, motioning at the big mess of rods as his eyes searched frantically. He grabbed a sheet of tin, threw it down.

She grabbed him by the arm, shook him, yelled, "Do you have any coal oil?"

"My God, coal oil?" He looked down at her from his increased height as though she had been drinking loco-weed tea or something.

"Yes, *coal oil.* You need to build a backfire," she told him in a rush of words, "away from your farm and toward the prairie fire. Soak a rope in coal oil, light the end and drag it behind your horse through the grass. Pray the wind turns. The burned over ground might stop the fire from burning you down." As well as her place and the town.

Most everybody else, herself included, had already plowed a fire-guard around their property. Two sets of furrows were plowed two or more rods apart and on a calm day the grass between was burned, creating the fire-break. But extra measures were always needed. A fiercely burning fire could jump a break, jump a creek or river, and keep burning. Anyhow, at Reilly's place, there wasn't time to plow a break, a back-fire was the only possible help and that chance small what with high weeds all over the place.

He sent the big bony dragon-fly one last panic-stricken gaze as though it was a living thing threatened by mortal danger, then he ran after her outside.

Exasperated and in a hurry to be away, she told him after she had swung into the saddle, "Your grandfather had some fine carpets. Wet them down if there's water in your well, and cover that—that *thing*. But first take care of your animals. Turn your horse and cow loose. I have to go on to the fire." She touched her heels to her horse.

Behind her, Reilly shouted, "Thank you for warning me in time. I'll do what you said. Will help come?"

"Likely," she yelled back, and slapped Taffy's sides with her reins. Every man, woman, and child for miles turned out to fight fire. It was an unwritten law meant to save lives, homes, livestock. If there was enough help at the line, she'd come back and see what she could do for Reilly. It would be good to be close to home if the fire came that far.

Someone in town had spotted the fire; she could hear the distant clanging of the old windmill bell, the pealing of church bells giving warning, calling people to battle the fire, save the town. Some of the tension in Lucy Ann's shoulders eased and she uttered a small prayer of gratitude. From her place, Paragon Springs was just a small cluster of buildings hugging the prairie to the southwest, but there would be activity there answering the threat of fire.

Paragon Springs was still county seat but in no way was it as prosperous as it had been in the boom years of the 1880's. The damage done the town by the depression and the Cherokee Run in 1893 when so many left, still showed. The population had decreased to around fifty and the place could almost be considered a ghost town. Funds for keeping up the streets, and for other services, simply weren't there. Many of its buildings were empty and boarded up. But farmers depended on commerce there and she had family and dear friends living in town still.

Although the winds of fate had blown ill time and again, devotion to their town was as strong as ever in its leaders. Her good friends, Aurelia and Owen Symington, Meg and

Hamilton Gibbs, and she had fought for the place from the time she, Meg, and Aurelia, lived together in a dugout. Desperate, determined young women trying to find ways day by day just to survive. They had succeeded by turning their homestead into a roadranch, a resting place for travelers, and later by building a town practically with their own hands. Hope for progress and the town's future were undying constants. They would never give up on Paragon Springs.

She considered riding there, to help prepare the town against the fire, figured plenty of others closer to town would have the same idea. So, instead, she kept riding hard toward the fire itself. As she drew closer she could see the writhing flames. In no time, smoke began to burn her eyes, ashes filled her throat. Jack-rabbits and birds on the wing and on the ground, rushed by in the opposite direction. Loose cattle and horses rumbled over the ground like thunder. They might run as far as the Arkansas River. It would take days to gather up missing stock, but it was better than having them dead.

As she had known folks would, as she had seen them do many times in the past, they were arriving from every direction, bringing with them every sort of fire-fighting apparatus imaginable to help put out the blaze. Barrels of precious water rocked in fast approaching wagons. Up and down the line folks rushed to unload sacks and blankets which they would wet down and use to beat the flames.

She spotted her son-in-law, David Thorne. In recent years he had filled out into a stocky, handsome man. He was a quiet sort, but hard-working and dedicated to Rachel and their children. She rode over to him. He and Rachel lived on her and Ad's old place outside Paragon Springs, buying the farm back from the man who bought it from them when they made the Run. In answer to the look on her face he nodded and told her, "Rachel and the young'uns are fine. I wasn't needed in town so I came on up here. You be careful, Ma."

She had finally gotten used to her son-in-law calling her *Ma*. For years she had been *Aunt Lucy Ann* to him, though they weren't really related then, just close as kin.

She nodded by way of answer. Before them flames roared, crackled, snapped. Even from yards away the heat felt like it would burn a person's skin off. Taffy trembled and pranced nervously beneath her. Lucy Ann spoke to her softly, patted her neck, and rode her away from the fire. Dismounting, Lucy Ann looped the reins around a wagon tongue. She swiftly retrieved a blanket and joined the others at the line, beating at the fire.

"Lucy Ann!" she heard someone call. She turned to see Meg motioning to her from where she stood in one of the water wagons. "I can use your help over here."

She hurried over and climbed aboard the wagon. Meg told her in a husky, smoke-choked voice, "I need your help to soak the blankets and pass them down to those using them in the line. We can't waste water," Meg's silver-gray eyes were worried, "or we'll run out. Grab the other end of this wet blanket and we'll wring it out enough to leave it wet, but not dripping water where it isn't needed."

Meg was often the first one of the trio of friends to conceive a new idea. She was taller and thinner than Lucy Ann; but had aged with the rest of them. At the moment, her salt-and-pepper pompadour was catching bits of ash from the wind, her shirt waist and trim gored skirt were wet from spills.

"Things are all right in town?" Lucy Ann panted as she took a hard grip on the blanket and twisted.

"So far. Bethany and Will Hessler have organized folks to see to precautions against the fire there. Aurelia and I thought we'd come and try to stop the fire before it burns further."

In a while, Aurelia moved from the line to help them. Her face was blackened with soot that settled in the creases around her mouth and eyes. Always a hard-worker, one wouldn't have known she was past sixty from the spry way she climbed into the wagon to take her station wetting sacks and blankets and passing them down to the firefighters.

The blankets, light before they were wet down, were extremely heavy when soaked. Lucy Ann's arms ached from the heavy work but she didn't slow. Her hair came loose to blow in her face like graying cornsilk but she paid it little mind. Around her, chains of friends and neighbors of all ages worked at a frantic, steady pace, fighting back the flames that threatened to advance and devour everything in its path.

The grim struggle continued for an hour, then two, three, four. A cry went up when in late afternoon the wind died to a mere whisper. Hopeful comments ran up and down the line, maybe the fire could be beaten yet. In another hour, the worst of the fire had been put out.

In the early evening, riders rode back and forth, dragging wet cowhides over last smoldering side-fires to put them out. Some of the men would spend the night along the line, watching and plowing under a wide break. Supper would be brought to them by the women preparing now to return home. There would be plenty of chores at their home places, but nearly everyone walked with a lighter step for having put the fire out.

The land, as far north as the eyes could see, was as black as a bucket of pitch. Bits of ash and fluff filled the air, cinders were hot underfoot. But the worst of the danger was over. Tired, glad, congratulatory shouts sounded up and down the line. There was laughter, releasing tension. Lucy Ann hugged Meg, and Aurelia. One more time, they had won, this time with no lives and no animals lost that anyone knew of.

Lucy Ann found David. "Looks like the danger's past," she said with a tired but relieved chuckle. "Give Rachel and the children my love and you all come over for supper soon."

"Sure, Ma." He grinned a white-toothed grin from his blackened face. "You all right?"

Lucy Ann nodded. "I'm fine, although I feel worn to a nubbin and you can see I'm covered with wet grime." With a last wave to Meg and Aurelia and her other friends, she climbed on Taffy and headed home. Sometimes her fifty-year-old bones let her know she wasn't as young as she used to be. She rode slowly, contemplative.

Tom Reilly's place, as she rode past, stood as always, rundown but safe. His horse and cow, grazing deep in the poorest pasture she had ever seen, lifted their heads as she passed. There was no need to check on Reilly and his silly contraption, and she was too tired to stop to say all was well.

Since the fire had been stopped miles from her place, her animals hadn't been threatened. For the most part they had stayed peacefully close to home, even with gates open they hadn't grazed far. She rounded them up, herded them to where they belonged, then locked the gates, closed up the pens.

Chores finished, she returned to her spic and span house where she warmed a scant quarter tubful of water for a bath. She clucked over small holes burned through her dress. The old lavendar calico's best days were about over anyway, she decided. She used her large bar of Fels Naptha laundry soap to wash away the grime in her hair, and from her body. Dressed again in clean clothes, she cooked a light supper of scrambled eggs and tea.

At first, she didn't realize how badly she was shaking. And when she did, she put it down to being so tired, of working all day. Which pretty often she could do, with no harm.

She looked around the room, close to tears with gratitude that her home still stood, the same as ever. So much more *could* have been destroyed today, if folks hadn't joined from far and wide to fight the fire.

She remembered her tin box of papers she had buried outside. No need to do that, as it turned out. She thought about leaving them where they were until morning. Then she decided maybe that wasn't a good idea.

Later, she spread papers from the box out on the kitchen table. One document was crisp and smelled new. It had arrived only a short time ago and she was still trying to figure it out. The document belonged in the bank, but then everyone would know about it and she wasn't ready for that yet. She still found it hard to believe that this had happened to her.

Anyway, who was to say the bank wouldn't have burned today if the fire hadn't been stopped? Or that it wouldn't be robbed as it was last year when one of those southeast Kansas outlaw gangs hit town?

Another of her papers was a small grubby wine-colored book, her husband, Admire's diary that he had written in before he was killed. She caressed the little book, felt a tide of emotion sweep over her. Admire had wanted to record every minute of the Cherokee Run, the greatest event of his life. As it turned out, the Run was also his last adventure. After all this time, every so often she liked to re-read the diary as a means of being close to him.

Some of the lines she knew by heart. "Sept. 5th. Have sold my Hodgeman County farm. Left today for Kiowa, Kansas with wife and daughter and a wagonload of provisions. Will take new land in the Strip."

Later entries after their arrival at Kiowa weren't so confident. "Sept. 12. I fear for my family. Heat is bad. Hardly no water. They been days camped at the town with thousands of strangers."

"Sept. 13. Last night I slept in line to the registration booth with 10,000 other men. How can there be land enough if this is how it is at them other border booths? I hope I ain't made a fool mistake."

The morning of the 16th his enthusiasm had returned. "I got my registration and flag. Everybody in line up early to wait for the signal. Lucy Ann come to the line and brought me breakfast. Lord, it was good to kiss her. Today I get our land. I am ready."

That morning she took him breakfast on the dusty waiting line was the last time she saw him alive.

Her hand trembled as she picked up the other, secret document. She shook her head. Did Ad, in heaven, somehow know what was in it? She wished he knew. Wished he were there with her to study what took place.

Chapter Six

Lucy Ann had always felt blessed that Ad wanted her for his wife. But if a plan she once had had been carried out, she would have been dead, cold in the ground, months before they met. They would never have known one another. They would never have had their mostly good wedded years together.

If there had been anyone *family* to raise her younger brother, Laddie, after the Sioux renegades savaged her, she would have taken her life. But Uncle Ross was their only kin and after she got to Kansas and found out he was dead she couldn't leave Lad alone. She was purely glad she hadn't shot herself. What good would it have done? And what an awful sin in God's eyes taking her life would have been!

What the Indians had done to her, and that Rachel was born from seed of that attack, had bothered Ad more than any of their best friends ever knew, more than he wanted it to bother him and more than Lucy Ann wanted to note.

Thinking of it caused Ad's occasional moodiness and sometimes he drank too much with his cowboy friends. He lamented many times, "If I could've just been there, I'd have killed them red devils myself on the spot." Although he loved her, he didn't lay with her as much as he might have otherwise. The rarity of those times in bed, she believed, was the reason she never had another child.

The only way she could put thought to the rape, herself, was to believe that the outrage happened to some other girl, not her. Most of the time, it seemed that way. Other times, she felt so dirtied, so soiled. Though not enough to die, once she had decided she had to live.

For all Ad was troubled, he did love her and he stayed by her. Their marriage was as good as some that didn't have such a burden of trouble taken into it. She wanted another child, Ad's child, so much. Not blessed that way, she had poured her love and attention on Rachel, on her brother Lad, and of course, on Admire.

She never fooled herself about her real reasons for accepting Ad's proposal of marriage. She knew deep in her heart no other man would want her if they knew of her past. She wanted a father for her baby daughter, half-Sioux or no, and as normal a life as possible for her young brother, Lad. But what began as gratitude toward Ad, had over the years become a deep and abiding love. She was sure he had felt her love for him.

She picked up the diary again and held it close to her breast. Her eyes filled anew.

He had had such great hopes for that new start. He had successfully staked his claim in the Cherokee Outlet only to be murdered for it.

The first years back in Paragon Springs after his murder were very hard for her. She missed Ad, his always being there beside her in their bed come night, being there by day when she needed his strength. She missed their talks, the warm, comforting sound of his voice, the feel of his touch.

For a time after her return she was forced to live on the charity of friends. Her brother, Lad—*Leonard* as he wanted to be called after he became a professional lawyer—helped her when he could. His law practice with Hamilton Gibbs, Meg's husband, brought in a little money, mostly from cow or horse thievery cases, disputes over land and debts, much of the country at that time was in a depression.

Lad had always shared a special bond with Lucy Ann's friend, Meg, and later, of course, with Hamilton. Lad had saved Meg's life when he was only twelve and she a young woman of twenty or so. She had fled to Kansas from St. Louis and her abusive first husband. Her husband had sent a bounty hunter to bring her back; Lad came upon him beating Meg. To save her life he was forced to shoot the bounty hunter. That had been part of earlier bad times, back in the 1870's. They had always been a close-knit community, like family, never hesitating to help one another.

Those days after the Strip Run, she took in sewing, did nursing and cooking for other people—when the work was available. Usually she bartered her work in exchange for her few needs.

The land courts in Oklahoma said they would look into Ad's rights to the Cherokee Strip claim and investigate his murder, speak with witnesses. But for a long time she heard nothing. It took almost four years for the courts to investigate Ad's case. She received word one day that they had ruled in Ad's favor. He was the legal claimant on the quarter-section he had staked out. His murderer was sentenced to jail and was killed in a shoot-out as he tried to escape punishment for his deed.

As Ad's widow, she was beneficiary of his claim. She hadn't wanted to leave Paragon Springs, so when his cowboy friends, who had taken claims adjoining his, asked to lease her land as part of their cattle spread, she agreed.

From that day, she received a small amount of "lease money" each year. Her difficulties trying to make a living eased. She was able, finally, to buy her small farm. Since then, she had lived frugally, quietly, in comfort enough to satisfy her. If sometimes she was lonely, a few hours extra work on her farm put an end to that.

She could have lived that way til her last days if this latest document hadn't put a different light on everything.

Oil. In recent months oil was discovered on Ad's land, *her* land, although she always thought of it as his. He was the one who had died for it. Investor-type men, for a share, had put in two or maybe it was three producing wells. She grappled with the fact that she was rich and found it hard to believe.

The money, as such, down there in an Oklahoma bank, wasn't that important to her. She really wouldn't know how to spend it. Oh, there were little extras it might be nice to have, like a sewing machine, or one of those new-fangled talking things—a telephone. But the truth was for the most part she was content with what she had. There was less bother to a simple life.

After giving it night after night of thought, she knew what she wanted to do with the money. She wanted to revive Paragon Springs. Not just give their town an exciting but temporary breath of life that would be gone in a whoosh, almost as soon as it had come as had happened so many times in the past with the arrival of numerous factories.

No, she wanted an industry that now and far, far into the future would provide work, guarantee an income for its resident folks. In particular for her friends of many years, and for her family. Something, or more than one *something*, that would make Paragon Springs the permanent, thriving town all of them—her women-friends with whom she had helped build the town, and their men—always intended it to be.

Meg, the one with the grand ideas, would have suggestions how to save the town with the money, she was sure. Aurelia, who led the way in building the town and who had nourished it all these years with her leadership against terrible odds, would have some ideas, too. So would Leonard, who was very smart, an excellent lawyer.

The welfare of his hometown would always be important to him, although of late he worried more and more that he would have to move his lawyering to Topeka. He already spent three months of the year there, serving in the legislature as Hodgeman County's elected representative. He could devise a plan, no doubt.

Besides his law practice, a small farm, and politics, he and his wife, Selinda, had taken over the Paragon Springs *Echo* newspaper after Selinda's mother, Emmaline, had retired from printing it. Selinda wrote as many articles and editorials as Leonard did and she sketched the art work. They had in recent years built the paper up into the *Tri-County Echo*, covering a much larger area of western Kansas. Their progressive paper was turning into the most popular newspaper in that part of the country, was housed in a fine new building on Main Street. She believed the pay was hardly equal, though, to either Selinda's or Leonard's talents. They were meant for great things, probably belonged in a thriving city with a large population.

She wanted to see Paragon Springs become that city, so they wouldn't have to leave, could stay in their hometown.

There were times lately she felt guilty for not telling even her own brother about the oil money. But keeping it secret was only for the time being. Only until she could make up her mind, *herself,* how to use the money to help everyone.

She had always known how others saw her: she was sweet, simple, quiet Lucy Ann Walsh with hardly a mind of her own. That wasn't and never had been the whole truth of who she was, the sort of person she really was. What the savages did to her when she was so young formed a shell around her which others saw as shyness. She was always

afraid—no matter how she behaved or how clean she was—
that the *taint* showed and that people could tell what had
happened to her. Nobody had ever really known the true
Lucy Ann, inside. Not even Leonard nor Ad. Not Meg or
Aurelia or any other of her friends. Truth to tell, she didn't
always know herself. She only knew that now she had the
chance, she wanted to do something big, really big. On her
own.

Fortunes had been poured into towns like hers, and lost,
over and over. Not this time. She would make the best effort possible, and it would be her decision. If it took a great
deal of time to decide, so be it. She had always been careful
with money, and she meant to be careful now.

Chapter Seven

The first week in May brought a delicious downpour of rain that lasted two days. Tiny weeds sprouted overnight in Lucy Ann's garden, then grew by leaps and bounds, faster than her vegetables. Crawling along on hands and knees, she pulled them out and tossed them into a bushel basket to give to her chickens.

She sat back on her heels for a moment, resting. The air was balmy and sweet, the sun felt just right. Feeling happy, she sang a few bars of an old song:

> *"Wake up, Jacob, day's a breakin'—*
> *Beans in the pot and a hoecake bakin'."*

Thinking about Jacob of the song who was sleeping when he ought to be up and about for work brought her thoughts of Reilly on the next farm. Not that he stayed abed late. Sometimes she saw him up and headed for the barn as soon as there was light to see by. At any hour of the night she might see lantern glow through his barn window and his house dark.

But he was still a slacker and a dunderhead to her mind, to spend so much time on the giant play-toy. Or was it some kind of weird art he worked on in his barn? The rain had caused the roof of one of his sod sheds to cave in and he'd done nothing to restore it.

She itched to tell him a thing or two and she might, soon. It might not be from criminal intent that he let that wonderful place fall to rack and ruin, but it still wasn't right. He could benefit from good advice, from instruction on how to manage better. And she wouldn't mind having a hand in the change, the improvement.

As it was, fury at what he was doing, or rather *not* doing, often disturbed her sleep at night and took her attention by day when she ought to mind her own work.

It was well after milking time one evening, she had finished her other chores and had returned to the house for supper. Her meal, tiny new potatoes creamed with fresh peas, and a wilted lettuce salad, was perfect to her liking. She had just sliced a piece of lemon pie when a knock sounded at the door. *Speak of the devil,* she thought, seeing through her kitchen window that it was her neighbor, Tom Reilly.

"Good evening, Mr. Reilly." He'd tied his horse by the well.

"Evenin'," he said, touching his gray hat. His booted foot, cocked on her bottom step, patted restlessly. Anger and impatience kept him from preamble. "Mrs. Walsh, have you seen my cow?"

"Seen your cow?"

"Damned old jersey got off somewhere and I can't find her!" He looked guilty for a second. "Excuse me for swearing, didn't mean to. She usually comes to the barn at milking time," he explained, scratching his jaw, "but tonight when I went out to milk she wasn't there. I rode all over the place looking for her, but I can't find her. She had a calf a few weeks ago. The calf's back at my place," he motioned with his head. "Thought maybe the cow wandered this way and you had seen her?"

"Sorry. No." *And if you kept your fences up this wouldn't have happened.* "If she's got a calf, she'll likely be back. She'll need to be milked."

He nodded, looked around him in the twilight. "She may be back there now." He turned to go. "Thanks, anyhow, Mrs. Walsh."

"Wait—" The chance was perfect to tell him some of the things that had plagued her mind. "Call me Lucy Ann, please. Most everyone does. Mr. Reilly, would you like to come in for a quick cup of coffee and a slice of lemon pie?"

"Lemon pie?" his eyes lit up, "I thought I smelled something good. You bet." His long legs took the porch steps up to follow her into the kitchen. "I should probably just get rid of that old cow. I could always buy milk in town or maybe from you," he said.

"Mr. Reilly, you haven't had much to do with a farm before, have you?" she asked as she placed his coffee and pie in front of him at the table. "Growing up I mean? Your people weren't farmers, were they?"

"Call me Tom. No, my father wasn't a farmer. He operated a stoneware company. My mother's only occupation was wife and mother. Both of them died when I was a baby. I was raised by my grandparents on my mother's side. I guess you could call Grandma and Grandpa Crane eccentrics. They loved one another but didn't live together. I lived most of the time in Wichita with her in a huge old house that looked like a castle. In fact, it was a castle—paid for with money from her ancestors' iron stove manufacturing company. House had twenty-eight rooms most of the time filled with fancy guests. Grandma's whole life was spent holding balls and tea parties and raising money for charities."

Goodness! Lucy Ann leaned forward and motioned for him to continue.

"Grandpa Crane, her husband, lived on a little farm over near Mount Hope. I spent summers with him. But I really didn't take to farming."

"No," she said politely but pointedly, "I suppose you didn't."

"Grandma Crane's high society way of life in Wichita didn't suit me, either. I loved my grandparents," he explained, "just not how they lived, either one."

He sounded spoiled, awful hard to please. Keeping her thoughts from showing on her face wasn't easy. She smiled and nodded.

"I learned my way around Wichita as a boy and when I wasn't in school, I spent my time at local machine shops. I made friends with the owners. They let me tinker, build things." He spoke fondly of that time, his eyes were shining.

She asked, "What about your other Grandpa, Eben Reilly? I don't recollect seeing you on his place until you came to stay."

He nodded, "Eben was my father's father. The two of them were estranged from an early time. Once in a while old Eben came to Wichita. I'd see him then, not often. I was surprised to learn when he died that he'd left me his place here in Hodgeman County. Didn't know what the hell I was going to do with it."

"It's a good farm!" This time Lucy Ann made no effort to be polite.

He failed to catch her meaning and he told her, "Then I realized that Grandpa Eben Reilly's place was perfect for what I wanted. Big barn. Wide open spaces. Strong south winds—"

"Oh, for heaven's sake!" she sputtered. "South wind! Open spaces! Big barn!" Suddenly, spelling it out that way, she knew what that contraption of his must be. It took her breath away. She clutched at her throat. "Mr. Reilly—Tom, are you building a—a flying machine over there in your barn? Something like the Wright brothers built at Kitty Hawk a few years back? Do you mean to go up in the air with that dragon-fly apparatus?" She sat back in her chair, astounded, and just a little bit concerned about his sanity.

"I'm building an aeroplane," he said confidently, "but when I'm finished it will be much better than those the Wrights built."

She agreed with most folks' thinking, that human beings weren't meant to fly, otherwise God would have provided them with wings. The aeroplane the Wright brothers built back in ought-three was a fluke, a silly toy. How could Tom Reilly throw himself whole hog into this pipedream and at the same time let one-hundred-sixty acres of prime farmland lie idle and neglected? How could anyone? If he understood farming, surely he would like it. She pondered that for a few seconds.

"How about you, Lucy Ann?" he asked suddenly, breaking into her thoughts.

He caught her by surprise. "What about—*me?*"

"You seem to live alone here. Your husband, Mr. Walsh—?"

"My husband, Admire, was killed in the Cherokee Strip Run in '93. Murdered." At his look of sympathy, she hurried on, "I have family. My daughter Rachel, her husband David and their children, Zachary, Marcus and Amy, are close by. Their farm is a few miles the other side of Paragon Springs. My brother, Leonard Voss and his wife Selinda— they have no children—live close by, too." She didn't mention that Leonard was quite well-known from his work in politics. Maybe Reilly would figure that out.

"You've been here all your life, then?" He sipped his coffee, looked at her over the cup's rim. He set the cup down empty.

"No, no, I was born in Nebraska. But that's enough talk about me." She jumped up, gathered their cups, plates and forks and took them to the wash-table. She glanced at him over her shoulder, determined to change the subject. "I hope your cow is home when you get there. It's not good for her to go for so long without being milked."

"Yeh," he nodded, "I hope she's back home, too. I'm too busy to waste time chasing the country looking for her. I may have to butcher and eat her, if she keeps running off."

"Or you could fix your fences!" she retorted. Anger brought warmth to her cheeks, her light blue eyes flashed. "That would keep her in." Of all things, to think of butchering and eating his milk cow rather than take time to mend his fence! He beat all, he really did. No farmer worth his salt would think of slaughtering a perfectly good milk cow. But then, he had made it clear he wasn't a farmer. She hesitated, then said, "Mr. Reilly—Tom, would you like for me to find someone to fix your fences? A boy from town who could use the work? I know a few who are very handy—"

He took his hat from where he had hung it on his knee and slowly unfolded from the chair to his feet. "You bet! If you know a youngster who could take the chore off my hands, send him over. I really don't have the time, myself, to fix fence, clean the henhouse, and do other tasks like that. Maybe you've noticed? My aeroplane—say, Mrs. Walsh, would you like to come over and let me explain my flying machine to you?"

She didn't hesitate to tell him, "No, I don't think so. My farm is small but it keeps me working from dawn to dark. I take time for church on Sunday, my quilting and suffrage clubs, and visiting family—other than that I'm very busy."

Lucy Ann felt a touch of guilt as she watched the light in Tom Reilly's eyes die, saw his disappointment in the fact that she had no interest in his nonsense-machine. She felt better when a smile broke across his face.

He said, amiably, "Well, just thought I'd ask. Thank you

for the pie, it was delicious. Only pie I've eaten that could come close in perfection was a piece of peach pie I had at Aurelia's Place, the restaurant over in town. The old woman there, Aurelia, said she's been serving pie in that same spot for more than twenty-five years. How about that? She's a hell of a good cook."

She winced. Her friend, Aurelia, would be surprised to be called an "old woman" even at age sixty-two, she thought, though she might seem old to Tom Reilly who looked about forty or so. "Yes, Aurelia is a good cook." And one of the handsomest, liveliest, hardest working women in that country. Reilly hadn't known enough of their kind of folks or he would have seen that for himself.

When Lucy Ann went out next morning to milk, Reilly's jersey cow stood outside her barn, lowing deep in its yellow throat to be taken inside with her animals. "You know a good place to be when you see one, don't you?" she said as she coaxed the cow into her barn with a palmful of grain.

The jersey's swinging bag was painfully distended and the creature moaned in discomfort. Lucy Ann milked her first, then went on with her own chores. She had barely finished and gone to the house to wash her breakfast dishes when Rachel and the two younger children stopped by on their way to visit friends who had a farm toward Ness City.

"Mama, I saw a jersey cow in your pasture," Rachel said when she came into the kitchen, her dark eyes flashing curiosity. "Why would you need two cows, or did you finally part with Brindle Bess?" She shook her head at Marcus and Amy who were eyeing first the stone cookie jar on the second shelf of the glass-front cupboard and then Lucy Ann's face. Rachel mouthed, "Not polite."

"Just so happens I have cookies, raisin-spice, for my

grandchildren." Lucy Ann got the jar down, enjoyed the anticipation on their faces. "There you are, sweet'ums." She gave each of them a hug with their cookie.

She couldn't be more proud of them. Marcus, eleven, and Amy, twelve, had their mother's dark eyes and hair, but were fairer-skinned, like David. They were normal, active, noisy youngsters, but their school-teacher mother kept a tight rein on them and made them behave none-the-less.

After the children thanked her and raced outside to play for a few minutes, Lucy Ann told Rachel, "I still have Bess. The jersey belongs to my neighbor, Mr. Reilly. His cow got out and wandered off from him, I'm going to take her home later this morning."

"Your neighbor, Mr. Reilly, is something of a mystery man, I hear tell," Rachel said. "Is he a hermit? He's been seen in town only a few times. You seem to be having truck with him, though. What is he really like?"

Lucy Ann started to answer that he was an "odd bird." Then, remembering that he wanted to fly, she started laughing and couldn't explain him at all. "I'm sure you'll meet him sometime," she said with a wave of her hand. "He's poor shakes as a farmer, I can tell you that." She finished filling her teakettle and set it on the stove. "Do you think the Davis boy would like to work for Mr. Reilly? He has a passel of chores over there needs doing. Work," she shook her head, "that he just ignores, himself."

The Davis family had lost their own farm, except for the small house they lived in and a small garden patch. Redhaired Joey, and his father, Lucas, a lean man, wiry and strong, took part-time work for other farmers when they could get it. They barely scraped by.

"You're helping that lazy-bones Reilly find someone to do his work?" Rachel was surprised. But she agreed that

Joey Davis was a good worker who needed the opportunity. Although she passed up Lucy Ann's offer of a cup of tea, she visited a while longer and then announced she had better be on her way before Marcus and Amy got themselves dirty playing out by the barn.

When the children answered their mother's call, Lucy Ann walked the little family out front to where Rachel had tied her driving mare and hack to the picket fence. Lucy Ann frowned when the sorrel mare began dropping a pile of steaming turds right by her gate.

"David is thinking about buying an automobile," Rachel told her with an excited smile as she climbed into the hack after the children and took up the reins. "He'll teach me to drive it when he does. Just think, Mama, on the worst of days I'll be able to drive our auto to school and be out of the weather."

She wanted to tell her that on the worst of days she probably wouldn't be able to get the auto out of the barn. But she shrugged and gave her a noncommittal smile. You couldn't tell young folks much. In their enthusiasm for something new and different they seemed to think they knew it all. Then of course, once in a great while, they turned out to be right.

Most young men she knew wanted an auto. She had heard that autos were common in larger cities. But in Hodgeman County they were still a rare and awesome sight. Most folks still preferred to use their horses, and often it took a team to pull an auto out of the mud when the vehicle got stuck. And afterward the farmer could still beat the automobile to town with his team, or so local farmers claimed.

"Your cow came to my place this morning," Lucy Ann told Reilly when she found him in his barn later. "She's tied up outside. I milked her and brought the milk over, too. Do you have something to put it in? I need to take my bucket back with me, my dishtowel, too. You'll need something to cover the milk with so the flies don't get in it." Flies were a great bother to her. They were dirty and nasty, always trying to swim in her pail of milk or do their business on her food. At home she swatted flies on sight, closed her doors quickly so they couldn't get inside.

She looked around the deep shadowy cavern of Reilly's barn. It was still a shock to be in a barn that had no stanchions or feed boxes, or the warm smells of hay, oats, sweet cow's milk and manure. Those were just a faint memory in this barn. It was a worse shock to see instead the huge artificial bird and have your nose offended by the smells of oil, metal, and glue.

He was working on his whatchamacallit, his aeroplane.

He looked over his shoulder at her with a glazed expression and a frown creased his forehead. He didn't like her interference, even though she had just done him a favor milking his cow and bringing the cow home. That set her teeth on edge.

"Mr. Reilly, I have a garden to cultivate at home. If you will just get me one of your buckets for your jersey's milk, I can get on back before the weeds grow higher than my potato plants!"

He seemed to wake from a dream, and he looked guilty. "I'm sorry! I shouldn't leave you standing there. Excuse my bad manners. Work on my aeroplane causes me to forget just about everything else. A bucket, I'll get a bucket. Oh, yes, and a cover for the bucket."

She followed him to his house where the exchange was made, his milk was placed in his kitchen ice box. "Please don't go," he begged. "Let me show you how my aeroplane works, I'd really like to."

"I have a lot to do at home—" she began. Still, she was curious. "You wouldn't get in it and try to—to fly off the ground?"

"No, it's not ready for that." It showed in his eyes that he liked it that she was even a bit interested. "But I'm getting very, very close. I'd enjoy telling you how it is going to work. Please—?"

He was like a boy, caught fast in a boy's dream.

She hesitated, then told him, "All right. If you will do something for me, Tom. Please, don't ever leave your cow so long without milking her. She suffered, and she'll dry up if she isn't milked regular."

"I would have milked her. She got out of her pasture and I couldn't find her."

"She got out because your fences are down in places, have holes big enough for an elephant to walk through. They need to be fixed." She went on fast before he could protest and tell her how busy he was, "I'm going to talk to young Joey Davis about choring for you. He's a good worker, he has worked for local farmers from almost the time he could spoon his own oatmeal. I'll see him this evening at his mother's house when our church ladies work on a quilt there. Do you want him to come over in the morning?"

"As soon as possible. Yes, please. And thank you, Mrs.—Lucy Ann."

"You're welcome. Now, show me your flying machine." She was glad he wasn't going to attempt to fly it, she wasn't ready to witness anything like that. Even if he managed to get his contraption off the ground, and she doubted he could because any fool could see it was lots heavier than air, he would crash back down and then what?

She followed him dutifully, politely, back to the barn, burying her anxiety to be home working where she belonged.

The double-winged, dragon-fly-looking contraption now had three wheels, one on each side under the bottom wing, another fastened to a rod stretched way out front. The wings had been covered with canvas since she saw the apparatus last. And there were flippy-flappy flag-like objects far to the front and far to the rear, fastened to metal rods.

"See," he said, "my aeroplane is a lot like the pusher-type Curtiss Golden Flyer." She nodded as though she knew exactly what he was talking about. "It's a biplane," he said, "two sets of wings, the action forced from the rear."

"I see."

"I call it the Blue Hawk."

She hid a smile. "It has a name?"

"Yes." He repeated proudly, "The Blue Hawk."

He walked around it, chest thrown out. "Pretty big, isn't it?" He said proudly before she could agree, "The Blue Hawk is thirty-nine feet nose to tail and thirty-two feet wing-tip to wing-tip. Its power comes from this sixty horse-power, water-cooled Hall Scott V-Eight engine." He slapped an ugly lump of metal the size of a new calf that was fastened on a metal bar close behind a little rack-like seat. In front of the seat was a dinner-plate-size wheel for guiding the thing. She tilted her head. Compared in size to the rest of the contraption, the seat looked like it was for a child. There was nothing more to keep him in it, keep him safe from falling?

"It's so open," she said, of the web of pipes and delicate fabric-covered wings. "Nothing to hold you in the seat. The wind could blow you to pieces." *And that providing the contraption left the ground at all!*

"Nah, I'll stay in." His face shadowed. "I need a bigger gas tank, though. Right now it only holds four gallons. Can't go very far on that." His expression warmed and she could see that he wanted to go high and far, to *fly*.

She stared at him a long time, her eyes wide and blue. There was something in his expression, his manner, that said for all the impossibility, he really was going to make it happen. Somehow. The knowledge that he knew what he was doing and would succeed, purely stumped her. For a long time she couldn't say anything, but she followed him about as he went on explaining.

"Thank you for showing me your aeroplane," she told him later, "I liked seeing it." It rather surprised her to realize she meant what she said, and then some.

One day Lucy Ann looked out her kitchen window and was startled to see Reilly's aeroplane outside his barn, sitting in the middle of his far field. She clutched a hand to her chest, wondering what was about to happen.

He had started to visit quite regularly, for pie, or hot bread with fresh butter. He seemed to know her baking day. She gave him farming advice, he gave her reports on his aeroplane. But he hadn't mentioned he was going to move the aeroplane from the barn. Realizing what that might mean, she began to worry.

From that distance, the Blue Hawk looked much smaller than it did in the barn. And a lot more fragile. How long had it been out there in the field? Was Reilly in the seat? She couldn't tell. As she watched, the contraption started to move, rolling faster and faster. Her heart climbed into her throat. She strained forward, her hands grabbed the windowsill. The aeroplane went up, up, a few feet, and then came back down. "Oh, Lord!" she yelped out loud. The aeroplane made two more hops, like a jackrabbit, then stopped and didn't move again.

She felt gripped with fear, yet thrilled. Tom Reilly's aeroplane had flown, almost. As her breathing returned to normal, she saw two tiny figures hopping up and down over there. They were Tom and his new hired boy, lean, red-haired Joey Davis. She clapped her hands for them, although they couldn't hear her yelp of glee. His apparatus had practically *flown.*

Chapter Eight

In the summer months that followed, Lucy Ann tried to become used to witnessing Reilly's hair-raising efforts to get his aeroplane to leave the ground and stay in the air. On take off, the wings would tilt this way and that way as it lifted for a few yards. Next, down it came with what had to be a bone-jarring thud that caused her, on the next farm, to cringe and cry out.

She would see him, with Joey's help, tow the aeroplane back to the barn where he would tinker with it for a few days, and then make another try.

In spite of weeks and months of trying, Reilly hadn't really flown for any length of time or distance. Against her will, she stopped her work to watch. The hip-hopping aeroplane was too strange a sight, too startling, too out of place in farm country not to notice. A team of mules and a farmer cutting hay was a sight she could see and never know she saw it. The aeroplane was another matter altogether.

Joey turned out to be a godsend working on Reilly's place, as she had known he would be. The trouble was, the work had piled up for far too long, and Tom was as apt to ask Joey's help with the aeroplane as with farm work. It was taking a while for Joey to make any headway as he attempted to mow off weedy fields, plow, put in late grain crops, and mend fence. His Pa might have helped, but he was working for somebody else, a farmer who was sick and would take back his work when he got well.

She gave Joey a hand when she had the time and energy from her own farming. But it was a busy time for her, too.

The first of her garden was coming on and she was trying to put as much of it by as she could. Her broomcorn was nearly ready to cut and shock, then the wheat.

By midsummer, nearly everyone in that country had seen Reilly's "winged jack rabbit" hopping higher and higher across his fields only to thump nose down. He and his "Blue Hawk" had become a laughing-stock. Paragon Springs's other newspaper, the small *Kansas Bulletin* printed article after article of teasing ridicule. The humorous columns increased the tiny *Bulletin*'s circulation to a degree that the editor, E.C. "Easy" Osborne, believed the day was near when his paper would be strong competition to the *Tri-County Echo*.

It wasn't surprising when a group of local men convinced Tom that he should demonstrate his flying machine at the Hodgeman County Fair in late August.

He had to know they only wanted to make fun of him, turn him into a spectacle. Still, he took on the matter as seriously as gospel on Sunday, and worked hard to be ready for the "big day."

The fairgrounds were located on the far west side of Paragon Springs, not far from the Santa Fe tracks. Approaching town from the northeast in her buggy, Taffy's reins loose in her hands, Lucy Ann thought to herself that even with all the changes, her old hometown was as familiar to her as her kitchen and backyard. Town was just more shabby and rundown. Dust blew everywhere.

On the east end, paint peeled from the hotel barn and freight office though they still operated. Murphy's boarding house and the bakery building stood forlornly empty for lack of business. On the other side, shabby but dignified, was the sheriff's office and home, Doc McLean's place, and the community bank. The bank suffered a couple of failures but was operating again for the time being.

On the north side of Main there was another drugstore on the lot where in the early days a profiteer and dealer in illegal whiskey, Boot Harris, had his so-called pharmacy. The later drugstore belonged to Doc McLean; he operated the rest of the building as a hospital. Where the old Yellow Rose dance hall used to stand was Aurelia's opera house, boarded up for now. Then the Marble House Hotel, owned by Bethany and Will Hessler and still hanging on, Aurelia's Place Restaurant, and the Jones' Drygoods Store.

Wurst's store was still open, although a son ran it most of the time now that Oscar was getting on in years. Most of the other businesses on the southside of main, except for the *Echo* offices and Pickering's blacksmith shop and livery, were 'temporarily closed.'

She tried to picture the town as it would look, revived, but was distracted by the sights and sounds of the fair as she approached. From the number of buggies, wagons, and horses, nearly everyone in the county had come for the day's celebration. She tied Taffy to the rope hitchline with the others.

She weaved through groups of racing, laughing children and yapping dogs. Past pens of noisy stock animals there for showing and to win ribbons for their owners. The air was filled with a delicious aroma of sizzling sausages and kraut, fried apples, and fried bread. Dazzling the eye with color were booths displaying canned vegetables and fruit, quilts and other handiwork. Last year she had won twenty-five ribbons for her entries, this year she had declined to enter.

At another booth draped in red, white, and blue, Leonard and two other Western Kansas legislators listened to folks' worries and concerns and answered their questions.

For the past four years, Leonard had been part of a group within the Republican party which had taken on the task of reform in Kansas, a movement originally spearheaded by the Populists, "the People's Party." They fought for reforms in state government and in laws concerning mortgages, labor, schools, corporations, land, taxation, and transportation.

She was particularly proud that last year Leonard's law to stop the sale of liquor for medicinal purposes had passed. Of course *enforcing* the law was as hard to do as stopping open saloons had been in earlier times.

He and the other two legislators in the booth were popular men in that country, but today they drew fewer people than usual at such gatherings.

By far the main attraction, although it had arrived late, was Tom's aeroplane. Joining a group of women-friends at the edge of the crowd, Lucy Ann stood and watched.

"Did you ever see the like?" Aurelia asked, with a doubtful shake of her head.

"You know," Meg said, eyes squinted shrewdly, her chin in her hand as she studied the scene, "I think an aeroplane might be a good idea."

Lucy Ann smiled, but remained silent.

Tom and Joey had brought the aeroplane to the fairgrounds on their hay wagon drawn by horses. There was no shortage of men to help unload the odd contraption. They jumped to, wearing huge grins and, as much as they were fascinated, they still made unkind jokes about Reilly's "turkey vulture" invention.

The demonstration was set for two o'clock in the afternoon. Somehow, Reilly had captured Lucy Ann's interest in his flying machine and she could hardly wait. Couldn't help hoping that this time, Lord, this time, the Blue Hawk would really fly. He had told her one time, "Getting my aeroplane into the air isn't so hard. It is getting it back down on the ground just right, that's the problem." On the day he told her that, thanks to a gusty wind he had flown the Blue Hawk five hundred feet into the air before coming down so roughly he by rights ought to have been killed.

He couldn't consider a flight successful, he said, until he both flew and *landed* smoothly. If he lived so long— she thought.

As she and Rachel spread blankets in the shade where they would have lunch, she muttered, "From all the talk I hear today, folks want to see Reilly crash, his blood splashed everywhere—"

"Oh, Mama," Rachel laughed, "they don't want to see any such thing. Folks do expect to see the man make a fool of himself. He has to be deranged to think he can fly in that—that whatchamacallit."

From under the brim of her sunbonnet, Lucy Ann leveled her gaze on Rachel. "It's an aeroplane," she said quietly, "and it is called Blue Hawk. I for one expect that Reilly will fly, and I hope he will."

All through lunch with Rachel, David, and the children, she felt Rachel's eyes watching her. "Are you feeling well, Mama? Aren't you hungry?"

"I had a big breakfast is all," she said untruthfully, setting her plate aside. Excitement and anticipation of Reilly's flight had done away with her appetite. Bless it all, she *wanted him to fly.*

Still, with all the talk, she began to feel embarrassed for Reilly. What if the Blue Hawk just sat there, or lifted a bit and tumbled to the ground, as it had so many times before?

She walked around after lunch with Leonard and Selinda. They seemed a bit more open-minded about the aeroplane than some; still, she could tell that they doubted Reilly would fly. Chiefly, for them, the event was a story for their newspaper, the expanded *Echo*.

Long before two o'clock a huge crowd had gathered at the far southside of the fairgrounds where the Blue Hawk sat.

Finally, Tom climbed into the seat. His flight instruments were a dollar watch fastened to the plane and a pocket barometer strapped to his wrist. Joey waved the crowd back, shouting that it could be unsafe and the two of them wanted nobody hurt.

Lucy Ann's oldest grandson, fifteen-year-old Zachary, his eyes glowing with excitement, was the last to move away.

There was a sudden silence from the onlookers as Tom's head lowered and he fiddled with the engine controls. There was a whir from the propeller in back, popping explosions from the motor. The wind was strong. The crowd moved back another step. The aeroplane began to move. Tom's gaze found Lucy Ann, he grinned and waved. The aeroplane rolled along and then there was a unified gasp as the contraption lifted into the air and *flew!*

Higher and higher the dragon-fly-looking machine climbed, silhouetted against blue sky and golden sunlight. Lucy Ann swallowed and followed the aeroplane with her eyes. The Blue Hawk with Reilly aboard was at least 700 feet up in the air, maybe higher. It leveled off, flew straight on, grew small in the distance. Then it turned slowly, circling back. The purring aeroplane grew in size as it flew closer. The only sounds from the crowd was an occasional pleased laugh, a comment, "He's up there, damned if he ain't!"

Zachary came to stand beside Lucy Ann. "What do you think of the aeroplane, Grandma?"

"I think—I think it's just stupendous, Zachary!"

For a second time, the aeroplane circled gracefully and with ease over the field. People began to clap, to cheer. As Tom came in close to the ground to land, he was buffeted by a strong wind. The Blue Hawk swayed wildly. Yet Tom kept control, skimming in close to the ground. In the excitement, nobody paid attention to the Santa Fe train until it roared by. It sucked the air from under Tom's aeroplane. His wheel touched ground and the Blue Hawk did a sudden flop over onto its back like a giant dead insect, Tom pinned beneath it.

There was one long gasp from the crowd before they plunged forward as one, yelling concern. A few men, silver-haired Owen Symington and Ham Gibbs among them, came quickly to their senses and waved the mob back.

Lucy Ann stared, wide-eyed and with a dry throat, wondering if he was dead. Wondering if his foolish boy-dream had killed him. She had wanted so much for him to fly, successfully. Worry tightened in her chest.

She was shorter than most of the crowd, and it was hard to see what was happening. But suddenly Tom was there, limping, rubbing his head, but alive. He threw up his hands and the crowd cheered wildly.

"Fool!" Lucy Ann smiled and muttered to herself, her voice shaking. "Fool!" She was happier for him than a woman with good sense ought to be, but she couldn't help it, and nobody would want to see him hurt bad.

The flip-flopped aeroplane was the topic of conversation for the next half-hour as the crowd milled around it. Several of the flying machine's ribs were broken, shafts were twisted.

The contraption had flown, though, they had all seen it. And if not for contrary winds, and the Santa Fe roaring by at the worst time, Tom would have landed it smoothly, too. Lucy Ann was sure of it.

Tom tied a handkerchief around his head to stop the bleeding. In spite of his head wound and his limp, he claimed he was all right. He collected a group of men who lifted the poor broken heap back onto the hay wagon.

Next day the *Tri-County Echo* pronounced demonstration of Reilly's Blue Hawk "awe-inspiring." Easy Osborne's *Kansas Bulletin* stated, "TURKEY VULTURE FLOPS TO GROUND."

Chapter Nine

As foolish as Lucy Ann now and then thought Tom to be, it was hard for her not to like him. Be fascinated by him. He was carefree and adventurous, and especially courageous, in what he wanted to do. He was good company on their visits back and forth. She felt younger, happier in their exchanges of talk, and ideas. Which in a way surprised her because she had been quite content with her slow and placid life before he came.

His talk, his dreams and goals when he shared them with her, left her spellbound. He explained again how an aeroplane, heavier than air, stayed *up there,* something she thought she might never quite grasp. "It has to do with *lift,*" he told her, "the force caused by the motion of air over and under the aeroplane's wings when it's moving. That pressure, greater below the wing than above, due to the wing's shape, pushes the aeroplane up. Forward movement is called *thrust* and the design of the wing and engine together causes that. Once an aeroplane is evenly balanced in flight it flies straight and true!"

"I see," she said, and she did, a little.

He told her, "I swear, someday a perfectly built flying machine will pass through air *for hours and hours* as easy and safe as we now pass over land and through the sea. The day will come when an aeroplane will transport mail and goods and people, quicker than anything else will ever be able to do."

She no longer had doubts that whatever he said would happen, could happen.

She was reminded that it had been difficult for most folks, herself included, to see how the auto could possibly replace the horse and wagon. Yet, amazingly, it was happening. Owen, Aurelia's husband, was one of those who at first vociferously cursed the auto as a weird invention that wouldn't last. Next thing she knew, he had turned around and sheepfaced made a place for an auto in his barn, putting his driving team out to pasture. Ham and Meg also had a new automobile.

Frank Pickering was thinking of turning his blacksmith shop in town into an auto repair garage, and maybe an auto sales store. The few folks around who owned autos now had to travel a far piece to have them fixed. It was the same to buy one.

And who would have ever thought you could talk across miles to friends or family as folks were doing more and more, by telephone? *There was a marvel for you, if there ever was one.* She didn't have a telephone, but some of her friends and neighbors did. She might get one, herself, before long. A person needed to keep up with the world, as long as the gadget wasn't something they truly minded, didn't like.

One evening in October when she had a pot of beef stew simmering on the stove, and biscuits baking in the oven, Tom showed up at her back door unexpectedly. She invited him to supper, they got to talking and she forgot all about her quilting meeting that night.

Rachel came over early the next day, an expression of unhappiness and concern marring her round, otherwise pretty face. While they visited about matters of little importance, Rachel pulled a lace handkerchief back and forth between her hands.

Lucy Ann was fairly sure what was coming, but she

waited for her daughter to get around to what she'd really come to discuss. In other words, why on earth would she miss a quilting party to gab with the likes of the birdman?

"Mama," she finally asked, "do you know folks are talking about you and Mr. Reilly? They are saying that you—well, you know, that you're—" her voice trailed off. Her dark eyes looked away with embarrassment. In another second her gaze came back to study Lucy Ann intently.

"Tom and I are what?" She felt her own face warming although she had no reason to feel guilty. She was doing nothing wrong.

"Keeping company. That you're a couple."

She laughed and shook her head. "Oh, honey, we're not a couple. Tom and I are neighbors, we are friends, but we aren't a couple. He is a lot younger than I am, and anyhow I couldn't ever feel that way about him or any other man. I loved your Papa. There could never be another man for me after Admire."

Rachel looked slightly less worried but still asked, "You're sure you're not just a bit smitten with him?"

"Smitten? Heavens, no, child! I told you, we are friends." She walked to the window, looked out at her tidy yard and fields. "Sometimes I get lonely. I like talking to him."

Rachel came up behind her, touched her shoulder. "He's a wild and silly man with a ridiculous flying machine. That you like him, would put up with him at all, surprises me, Mama. Folks enjoyed seeing the demonstration at the fair, but nobody really believes his aeroplane will amount to anything. You said yourself that he is a disgrace as a farmer."

She turned slowly, wished she could make her daughter understand. "Rachel, I'm sorry that it bothers you that I like my neighbor. But I do. And his aeroplane interests me.

He's rebuilding the Blue Hawk, you know, but better—"

Rachel didn't seem awfully interested so she dropped the subject. They talked instead about the quilts they were making, whether the apple trees Selinda and Leonard had set out on their farm might freeze and die come winter. As Rachel was leaving some time later, they walked out to the garden, mostly harvested now. Lucy Ann gave her some pumpkins for the children to make jack-o-lanterns, and some smaller pie pumpkins.

After Rachel was gone, she began to feel angry, and hurt. Why would anyone choose to talk about her? *Gossip,* was the correct word. She wasn't hurting a soul, least of all herself. She had probably been a little girl the last time she felt as excited about anything as she did about Reilly's dream. What was so wrong about that?

Leonard was so busy with his campaign, at his newspaper and on the farm, she saw little of him after the fair. Then he came one evening the second week of November when elections were over. He was pleased that Walter Roscoe Stubbs, a Republican like himself and known as "the fighting Quaker," had been re-elected Governor. Republicans had won all state offices and congressional seats, and sixty-two seats in the House.

She was glad to hear his news, was glad simply to spend a little time with him.

Time had brought only good changes to her brother, she thought. He still wore his sandy hair in a swoop down over his forehead to hide the old scars where the savages had partially scalped him. There was a sprinkle of gray in his hair and moustache, a few deeper lines around his eyes and mouth than used to be, which she thought lent him a handsome, dignified look.

"You make your sister very, very proud," she said, holding his hand as she congratulated him on his own re-election. She had never mentioned it before but it had crossed her mind and now she asked, "Will you run for Governor of Kansas one of these times?"

"For crying out loud—?" He looked surprised, puzzled. The smile lines in his face deepened, his eyes sparkled. "Why would you—What makes you ask?"

"I know you." She returned his smile, led the way into her kitchen, got out cups and saucers from the cupboard. She stirred the fire and put the coffee pot on. "I've always been able to read your mind," she teased. "I got plenty of practice during that time when you were a little boy and couldn't talk." For months after the Indian raid on their Nebraska farm, he had been mute. "Truly, though, you would make a fine governor for Kansas, Leonard. You're honest, you care about the people of this state, and are am-bitious for them. Kansas couldn't do any better and that's from someone who knows you very well."

His grin widened. "Thanks, Sister, I'll try not to keep in mind how very prejudiced you are where I am involved." He was thoughtful a moment as he leaned back against her pie safe. "I won't say the idea of being governor hasn't crossed my mind. But that would be far in the future. For now the platforms I favor, chiefly to advance the cause of progress in Kansas, will be more than ably enacted under Stubbs's hand as governor."

"Including woman suffrage?" For as long as she could remember, Kansas women had fought for betterment for themselves. They had made a few gains here and there, as in the right to own property, and the right to custody of their own children. But the right to vote in general elections was still not available to them.

"Of course including woman suffrage. You know I am in favor of women having the vote and I hope they get it. I'm just sorry the measure keeps failing, but that won't occur much longer, I promise you."

"I'm glad you're in favor, Leonard, and are helping us to push for the vote."

"Growing up with the women in my Paragon Springs family as I did, how could I feel other than I do? You've all convinced me, impressed me. Meg, Aurelia, Emmaline, my dear Selinda. As Voltaire said, 'All the reasonings of men are not worth one sentiment of women.' "

She chuckled with him, but added seriously, "I truly can't understand why women aren't given the vote. There are ignorant women, I'll admit, but there are also ignorant men. The other way around is just as true, there are women who are as smart as men."

In the course of the evening, as they sipped coffee in her small parlor, the subject of gossip about her and Reilly came up as she was afraid it might.

"I don't want to embarrass my family or myself," she told him. *Hadn't she made a career, practically, of trying not to offend, to be proper?* "I don't know what makes folks think the way they do. I don't feel I am doing anything wrong, honestly, Leonard, I don't. Tom likes my cooking, I enjoy his aeroplane stories. Sometimes I help him out of a bind when he makes some stupid mistake or other over there on his place. That's all there is between us."

He leaned forward, took her hand. "It's all right, Lucy Ann, you don't have to defend yourself with me. If ever a person has earned the right to do as she pleases, you have." He spoke emphatically, with warm affection showing in his eyes. "You've gotten some harsh treatment from life in the past, and none of it your fault. Whatever sort of happiness or enjoyment comes your way, dear Sister, you go ahead and grab it."

She blinked at a burning in her eyes. They rarely referred directly to the Indian raid of their childhood, what had happened to them, plus the loss of the rest of their family at the hands of savages. It was a subject too ugly and painful. Her voice was husky with tears gathering in her throat, "Thank you, Leonard, for feeling that way."

"Of course that's how I feel. I will always be indebted to you for raising me. You were like a mother to me after we lost Mama, and Papa. You were hardly more than a child yourself, then."

She made a small motion with her hand. "Leonard, there was nothing else—"

But he wouldn't let her interrupt his praise. "I can't ever thank you enough for encouraging my education, helping to pay for it. I know you went without so I could attend law school. I'm not sure I would have had the courage to enter politics, if you hadn't believed in me and encouraged it so. I love you, Sister, and I think you should do anything you please."

"What a speech, Leonard!" She shook her head then took a quick drink of coffee to help clear her throat. "But I do appreciate it."

"It was long over-due."

"Oh, posh." She put her cup down and smiled at him. "You've been thanking me regular since you turned into a young man and started using your good sense."

He laughed. "I suppose so. I should have, anyway."

She was glad that he appreciated what she had done for him but more than that she was grateful for the closeness they shared. She was happy that it would be that way for them all of their lives.

The next thing she knew she was breaking not only a comfortable silence between them but a vow she had given herself to wait longer, and was telling him about the oil money.

He was stunned and sat back in his chair to stare at her. "You're sure? Lucy Ann, you're not making a joke?"

"It is true, Leonard. I can show you the papers." She started to get up.

"They aren't in the bank? Good Lord, Sis—!"

"I know, I know. I'm taking a risk, keeping them with me. But for now I'm sure they are as safe with me as anywhere. I'm going to put them in a safety deposit box, soon. It's just that I don't want anyone to know about the money, yet. They can be gossipy down at the bank even if they're not supposed to be." She considered, "You can tell Selinda, she's your wife, after all, but please don't tell anyone else." She explained her intention to help the town with the money, adding that she wasn't sure exactly how she wanted to go about it, yet.

Leonard was still shaking his head. "So much money, are you sure you can handle it alone?" He gave a wry laugh. "I'm a lawyer, Lucy Ann. I could help you. I'm your brother, for Pete's sake."

"Now, Leonard, you know I trust you. It isn't that. I just want to do this myself. When I need your help, and I likely will, I'll ask for it. But in the meantime I just want to do this my way."

He stared at her with a bemused grin, then threw up his hands and rose to his feet. "All right, Lucy Ann. I said it before, and I'll say it again. Nobody ever earned more the right to do what they want than you have." He shook his head. "At the time I said it, though, I didn't realize there was so much money—Well, it is yours. And that's that.

Whatever you want to do for Paragon Springs—in your own good time and whatever you decide—you know I will support you."

She thanked him again. He left a while later, still looking like he'd been struck into shock by a Santa Fe train. But she knew he would stand by her, and he would keep his word.

Another thing for certain: as soon as Leonard shared the money secret with his wife, and Selinda could get away from the paper and her society work, she would be over. Lucy Ann was just putting the last bit of icing on a small chocolate cake next day when Selinda came. Selinda loved chocolate. It would go fine with their coffee.

Although she wore a worried frown, Selinda was as strikingly lovely as ever as she entered the small front parlor on a rush of cold air. "Hello, Lucy Ann." She removed her hat—which reminded Lucy Ann of a large gray platter of pink and gray satin roses—to reveal her black hair worn in a modish loose pompadour. Selinda wasn't extravagant, but her clothes were always well-made and in fashion. Today under her cloak, which she removed, she wore an empire dove-gray woolen dress with dolman sleeves and a fan collar. "Lucy Ann, can we talk please?"

"Of course. I have chocolate cake, and the coffee is on."

Chapter Ten

"Please let Leonard manage the money for you, Lucy Ann." Selinda's hazel eyes brimmed concern. "He didn't send me here to say that, believe me. In fact he said to let you be. I'm speaking for myself. Leonard says this is thousands of dollars, many thousands, that you have? And it is down in Oklahoma in a bank?"

Lucy Ann liked Selinda, they had always gotten along. But now she had to make an effort to be calm and hold her ground against her sister-in-law's probing solicitude. She nodded and smiled. "Yes, oil was found on Ad's land."

"Well, you have to let Leonard handle your financial affairs. If not him, Hamilton Gibbs. Or both of them together."

She answered softly but sure, "I don't have any 'financial affairs'."

"Yes you do, dear. You do! All this—this money. You need someone to guard it for you, invest it wisely." Selinda's concern was genuine. "You know I have always believed the world was made for women, too, not just for men. We women have rights, particularly the right to take charge of our own lives. But this is so—so different. This is too big a matter to handle alone. That's all I'm saying. The final word, in any event, would be yours. But you need help."

"You are right about one thing. The money is mine, to do with as I please. And I'm not ready to do anything at all with it, yet. When I am ready, my brother will be the first person I call on if I need him. In the meantime, I trust the people in Oklahoma I do business with. Besides, Ad's friends there, to the death, would see that I am treated fair and aboveboard."

"Well, thank goodness for that." Selinda looked relieved. "I wasn't going to say anything about it to you, I really wasn't. Leonard said you don't want anyone to know until you're ready and I can understand that. But then, I—I—"

"What?" She braced herself for what she guessed was coming. Selinda's other worry was going to be *Tom*.

"Well, I got to thinking about this fellow next door to you. Folks claim you spend a lot of time together. And the lunatic is building this flying machine, or trying to, and he doesn't seem to have an obvious source of money. He'll need plenty if he continues to try and improve that—whatchamacallit. The way he manages his farm can't be bringing in any more than food for his table, if that." She drew a deep breath. "You're all alone and now you have money."

"I don't think I like what you're saying, Selinda."

"I don't like what I'm saying, either, Lucy Ann," she answered truthfully in a stricken voice. "In a way it's counter to everything I believe. But I'm worried about you." She caught up Lucy Ann's hand in her long tapered fingers. "In this instance someone has to look out for you. You haven't had experience with a man like Tom Reilly. Word is that you have—taken him under your wing. You feed him, help him and his hired boy on that farm. In the blink of an eye he could talk you out of your money to help build his contraptions. Not to mention break your heart. You need to be careful—"

"I am careful." She withdrew her hand.

"Oh, Lucy Ann, I know. I know you are. But you aren't experienced in handling so much money, any more than you've had truck with people like Tom Reilly. Have you ever had more at one time before than a few dollars you could tie up in your handkerchief? I beg you to cut your ties with this fellow before it comes to anything more. And let Leonard advise you, take care of your affairs."

Selinda's usual views about a woman's rights hurt all the more because she believed Lucy Ann didn't have the good common sense to look out for herself. It angered her, yet she'd been aware for years how others judged her, or rather, misjudged her.

As she herself saw it, a person, man or woman, tidy in all other ways could be just as tidy handling money. Have every bit as much care in that area. She was neither a spendthrift nor a fool. She was old enough, wise enough, to choose her own friends.

"Selinda, I appreciate your worry about me, but it isn't necessary. I won't do anything foolish, I promise." *And please don't view me as crazy, the way all of you see my friend, Tom Reilly.* "Given time you'll see that there is nothing to worry about."

Selinda didn't look convinced. She hugged her tightly before she left. "It is your life," she admitted, her soft, well-modulated voice trying to sound accepting. "But don't let yourself get hurt, please."

It was a cold December day. Lucy Ann was out in the coal shed, filling a bucket with coal for her heating stove. She could hear overhead the soft drone of the Blue Hawk. It sounded like the gentle purr of a cat. She had thought Tom had put the aeroplane away for the winter. And of course he should have. He *was* a fool sometimes! It had to be freezing cold out in the open up there and dangerous to fly. But he seemed to have a fire inside that drove him into the air, as though the sky was his truest home.

She was halfway to the house with the coal when she realized the purring had become a raucous buzzing, a cough and then the sounds abruptly stopped. She dropped the coal bucket and whirled around to look. The Blue Hawk was low in the sky, but was descending too rapidly, straight down, like a large wounded goose.

She began to run. The flying machine struck the ground long before she was close. The awful sound rang in her ears like recurrent thunder, the quiet that followed was worse. It took forever to reach the pile of twisted steel and fluttering, torn canvas.

"Tom! Tom?" He was tangled in the heap, unconscious, his lower leg twisted at a terrible angle. "Dear God, Tom!" The mess of the Blue Hawk was too heavy, too unwieldy, for her to lift it off of him. She had to free him some other way. She took his shoulders, pulled. His injuries would need tending, she had to get him home somehow, get Doc Rod. She tugged again. The movement brought him pain, and the pain brought him to, screaming so that she had to stop.

"Don't," he begged. "Don't." He stared around him, bewildered. He saw then that he was wrapped in twisted metal and he closed his eyes. "No. God, no. The Blue Hawk. I remember now. It was too cold up there, I guess. I was nearly out of gasoline. The props must have froze up."

"Hush. You're alive. Don't say anything." A sound caused her to turn and Joey was there, bundled against the cold, racing hard across the field toward them.

"I was shucking feedcorn." He breathed hard, his words making small clouds of steam in the air. "I should have been with Tom. Is he all right? Tom, you all right?"

Tom had slipped into unconsciousness again.

"He's all right," Lucy Ann said, hoping he was. "But

he's got to be awful bruised, and his leg is broken. I need help. Grab that piece of broken rod there and use it like a crowbar. Put it right under here, where the mashed seat is, and pry up. As soon as you raise it, I'll pull him out." After the third try, she was able to drag him, a lead-weight against her strength, free. He was lucky to have fainted, otherwise she doubted he could have borne the pain.

She panted. "Get the wagon, Joey, and some blankets. We need to take him to the house and get him into bed. Then I want you to fetch Doc Rod, in town. Tom doesn't have a telephone yet, does he?"

Joey shook his head.

"Neither do I. Guess it is time we each got one. You'll have to ride to town for Doc Rod."

With Joey doing most of the lifting, they got Tom to the house and in bed. Then Joey rushed out to get Doc Rod. Tom was fading in and out of consciousness and she knew he had to be in great pain. Slowly and carefully, she slipped a pillow long-wise under his broken leg and tried to straighten the limb as much as possible. She winced at the sound of broken bone grating on broken bone. She found a kitchen knife and used it to cut open the leg of his trousers and long underwear up to his thigh. At the point of fracture, midway between ankle and knee, the limb tended to fall inward but the skin had not been punctured.

It was best to allow Doc to set and splint the leg. She hoped he would get there, soon.

She began to look for other wounds, had Tom half-undressed before she remembered that he was not her husband, Admire, and maybe it wasn't the proper thing to do.

He had a goose-egg bump on the side of his head, several cuts and bruises on his arms and chest. If he was hurt anywhere else, she would have to leave it for Doc. She put a cold wet cloth on the lump on his head, washed his face and exposed limbs gently with warm soap and water, dried him, then covered him carefully with blankets. Then she went to build up the fire so he would not get a chill. For herself, she needed a very strong cup of coffee.

"You've done half my job for me," Doc Rod commented later after he had given Tom an expert examination. "Thanks, Lucy Ann." She would have been glad to let him take over entirely but he wanted her help. "I am going to have to draw his leg down into its normal position. I will be putting gentle pressure, right here, at the seat of injury, in order to put the fragments back in their proper position. I'll need for you to hold his leg for me while I apply some soft tow pads and then splints."

Tom remained out while they set the leg. Afterward, Doc tinctured the rest of Tom's wounds, none of which he deemed serious. Tom had taken a severe blow to the head, but his skull wasn't fractured. He might suffer from headache, would need to take it easy for some time, but the broken leg was the more serious wound.

Tom, regaining consciousness but in pain, agreed.

It was decided that Joey, who had ridden back with Doc Rod in his auto, would spend the night. Tom ought to feel better by morning, although it would be many weeks before the splints would come off and he could use his leg.

When Doc Rod let her off at her gate hours later, the fire in her stove had been out for hours. Her house was cold as ice. There was no supper on the stove and she still had her chores to do. She had given Doc Rod her word that she would look in on Tom every day until he was better. Let him know if there was any change, otherwise he would come next week to check on Tom.

As if she had nothing else to do. Maybe she had taken leave of her senses. No, she was simply doing a kindness for a neighbor. As she would do for any neighbor, whomever the neighbor might be or how daft they might be at times.

Although she had strong doubts, Tom believed some of the wrecked aeroplane might be salvaged. Next day she looked out her kitchen window and saw Joey and his father, Lucas, hauling the wrecked heap of metal and tattered canvas into Tom's barn on the hay wagon.

During Tom's time abed, Lucy Ann and Joey prepared their farms for winter. They hauled and piled straw around the foundation of her house and Tom's to keep out the cold. Fresh supplies of coal were ordered. They got the last of the corn on both farms shucked and stored, and the corn husks packed in silage pits in the ground.

Sometimes she worked alone.

Rabbits had always been a problem in Kansas, gobbling up whole fields of crops before the grains could mature but that year wild rabbits had been worse than ever, had multiplied to an unbelievable degree. Farmers felt fortunate to have even part of a crop to put by.

Joey had learned he could earn seven cents for each rabbit he killed. He was often off hunting and one thing could be said, he was making fair wages. Tom, of course, was still house-bound but railing to recover, fast. He had begun work again on new designs for the aeroplane he hoped to perfect.

She invited him for Christmas dinner but he said hobbling around was too much trouble and he didn't want to "bust in on family." Late Christmas day when everyone had left, she saddled Taffy and rode over to Tom's with a

Christmas basket of leftover ham, corn pudding, and mince pie.

After he had eaten, she gave him a scarf she had knitted from royal blue wool. "It will make you look—dashing, when you're able to go up in your aeroplane again."

He seemed surprised but grateful. "I have a present for you, too." He got up and used his crutch to hobble over to his cupboard. He came back and handed her a tiny replica of a flying machine. The frame was carved from cottonwood, it was sleek and intricate and perfect. There were tiny wire controls and wing braces, cloth covered wings, wood propeller, rudders, tail skids, and landing gear, fingernail sized wheels. "I'm going to build the full-size version, with a few more improvements, but this model is yours. The rest of your present is that when the real version is built, I want you to name it. You can call it whatever you want."

She was a trifle embarrassed and didn't know what to say. She liked the flying machine, though, very, very much.

"Seems like you're always doing something for me, on the place, and now bringing me food and looking after this confounded leg. I'm going to be a long time repaying you."

"You don't have to repay me." She could have told him she felt already repaid by his friendship. A blessing she might not have the chance to enjoy if he knew much about her, about her past. She felt repaid by the excitement his aeroplane building had brought to her dull quiet life.

She looked down at the small aeroplane in her hands, wondering what she could tell him. It was beautiful and like nothing she had ever seen. "I'll put it on my mantel. And when the big one is built, I will try to decide on a good name for it." She smiled at him. "I have named a few cows and horses, but never an aeroplane. Thank you."

★ ★ ★ ★ ★

In mid-January, she was invited to Selinda and Leonard's for supper. Leonard wouldn't be able to join them personally as the State legislature had convened on the tenth and he was again in Topeka. Rachel, David, and the children were invited, though, and Emmaline, Selinda's mother. They stopped by in David and Rachel's large sleigh to pick her up for the drive.

It had snowed in fits and starts since Christmas and drifts were deep. Bundled under quilts and cowhide covers, they sped over the snow in the crisp night. Over their heads, stars were like millions of glittering diamonds in the inky sky.

It was a happy jaunt, and Lucy Ann settled her mind for a pleasant evening.

Leonard and Selinda's house was large and comfortable, Selinda's artful eye and good taste showed in every room. The meal that soon followed their arrival was sumptuous, bringing Lucy Ann to comment that Selinda had bested even such good cooks as herself and Aurelia, and of course, Rachel.

It wasn't long before Lucy Ann realized that the pleasant flow of conversation was being continually interrupted by questions directed to her about her neighbor, Tom Reilly. How was he? Had he given up the insanity of flying now that he had crashed? Any chance he would be leaving Hodgeman County since he was such a failure at farming and now had ruined his flying machine? What were his plans, anyway?

They knew she had been going daily to help out while he was injured. They wouldn't want to know that Tom was working harder than ever to perfect the design of his next flying machine and was constantly drawing new ideas. Despite his mechanical bent, he had had no formal training, so he was also working to complete a correspondence course in mechanical engineering. And he believed that right where he was, outside Paragon Springs, was the ideal place to test his inventions. He wasn't moving anywhere.

She told them none of that. Instead, she replied quick, vague answers, and changed the subject each time with whatever her mind could dream up. It was that or allow them the chance to persuade her to have little or nothing to do with him. And Tom was her friend, an enjoyable friend.

Doctor Rod had wanted Tom to stay down longer but nothing could keep Tom out of his machine shop and toiling over the destructed aeroplane as soon as he was able to move around. Joey set up a small heating stove in the shop. Hour upon hour, with his crutch leaning against his chair and tools in hand, moving the chair as needed, Tom dismantled the Blue Hawk piece by piece. He salvaged what he could for his new aeroplane.

Oblivious to the cumbersomeness of his splinted leg and whatever pain he might feel, and seemingly unaware that the small heater was no match for the frigid cold, his work continued steadily throughout most of the long winter.

When spring 1911 arrived, soft and balmy and greening, Tom was managing with only a bit of a hobble, although he used a cane on occasion.

"I think," Lucy Ann told him one day on a visit, "that we should plant milo maize this year, at least a small trial field or two. The Rock Island Railroad company is promoting it. They are saying that milo will be the 'salvation of the west.' It makes wonderful stock feed. And—I know now what to do with all that Russian thistle that has to be cleared off your fields. Stored for winter, it makes fair cattle feed so I'm told. I think you could get a half-ton of thistle to the acre and you have eighty acres."

"I don't raise cattle," he answered absentmindedly from where he studied some blueprint papers at his kitchen table.

"You could. Or you could sell the milo for a cash crop. You could give the thistle away free if you can't find anyone to pay for it. There are plenty of ranchers who could use it. I'm going to plant milo."

"Fine. I suppose I will, too. Lucy Ann, would you like to attend an airshow with me?"

Through friends also interested in aviation, he had heard that the Moisant International Aviators would be presenting a three-day airshow at Hutchinson in southcentral Kansas. The daring aerial acrobatics by the flying Frenchmen were not to be missed. Even the town's stores and schools would be closed for one of the show days.

In the past couple of years, he had witnessed several such shows and in part they were responsible for his interest in flying. "We can take the train, spend the day, return home the same night late."

"But I have so much work—" she mumbled as she considered his invitation. She remembered what he had told her about airshows he'd seen last year and the year before. It would be a thrilling sight, something she'd never seen before. Really, her fields were still too wet to plow. She could get Lucas to see to her other chores. "Thank you, Tom, I believe I'd like to go."

Hutchinson was a fair-sized city on the north bank of the Arkansas River. They left the train at Third and Walnut Streets, an area of neat shabby streets hugging close to the river and the railroad tracks.

They hired a hack and set off on their drive across town to where the airshow would be held, just beyond the eastern city limits. As they drove, they noted the numerous flour mills, grain elevators, and salt plants. Close to the business district of stone buildings two to eight stories high, were many fine homes with broad lawns, the impressive result of fortunes made in cattle, salt, and prairie real estate. Hutchinson was often called "Salt City" for the thick deposits of salt that lay under the city and surrounding country. Salt mines and plants employed most of the male population.

Many of the storefronts they passed were plastered with posters about the Moisant Aviators. The words, DAREDEVIL, DEATH-DEFYING, DIP-OF-DEATH, WING-WALKER, SPIRAL DIVE, leaped out. Her heart began to pound with excitement, and she was glad she had come.

There was a huge crowd as they approached the farm field east of town where the show was being held. They left their hack with the others and Tom caught her elbow and made a path for them through the crowd. She could sense his excitement, although his own dream of flying dealt with transport and commerce more than entertainment such as today's *birdmen* would provide.

The first biplane, to the cheers of the crowd, was in the air almost immediately, taking off from the field little more than twenty-five feet from the starting point. The first stunt was a full circle loop-the-loop. "It takes the flyer maximum throttle to achieve that vertical lift," Tom yelled explanation to her against the noise of the crowd.

A second aeroplane took to the air. That flyer showed off downward spins that made the entire crowd draw its breath in unison. There were barrel rolls side to side, turns in ninety-degree increments. The first aeroplane was then

107

doing a whip stall that stopped the plane vertically in the air. "Did you see that?" Tom asked on a explosive breath. She had, but she could hardly believe her eyes. "It hung there," she answered him, "the aeroplane just hung there!"

At lunch-time, he bought them roast-beef sandwiches and lemonade and asked if she would like to take a ride in one of the aeroplanes. The exhibitors were offering rides for one dollar. "No," she told him, "not this time. But you go." She would have been terrified, though she didn't say so. She loved seeing the aeroplanes though, couldn't stop marveling at the spectacular feats.

While she ate her sandwich her eyes were on the skies and the French biplane carrying Tom. It made some mild swoops, but mostly flew straight for several miles over the farmland, circled a bit, and returned.

The afternoon brought more "death-defying" air stunts. The maneuvers of the aeroplanes made her think of ocean waves, which she had only seen in pictures, and dropping leaves in the fall. Her stomach began to churn. Later, one flyer's partner stepped out on the aeroplane's wing. He danced nimbly there. Then, while the crowd held its collective breath, two of the planes flew close together and the dancer leaped from the wing of the first plane to the wing of the second.

The crowd roared its pleasure. Lucy Ann could only shake her head. In all her life she had never seen a sight so daring, so exciting. In the finale of the day, a man in a clown suit leaped from the aeroplane only to have a sudden *something* billow out behind him, like a cupped bedsheet. Lucy Ann clutched Tom's arm, she stared wide-eyed, knew she was seeing the unimaginable, she could hardly breathe. She managed a scream, "He'll be killed!"

"No, he won't. That white cloud apparatus attached to

him is his parachute," Tom shouted to her above the crowd noise. "He'll float down easy." He didn't sound certain, though. He didn't clap until the clown was safely on the ground and was handing out candy to the crowd swarming around him.

On the way home on the train she couldn't stop talking about all the stunts they had seen but particularly the marvel of the parachute. "I don't think I'd ever heard of a parachute before, but you knew about it." Of course he would, having gone to other shows.

Beside her, he nodded. "I learned about parachutes the hard way."

"What do you mean? You've never leapt from a plane with one, have you?"

He proceeded to tell her that when he was several years younger, he had allowed himself to be shot out of a hot air balloon by a cannon. "The parachute was stuffed into the cannon. When the balloon was up a thousand feet, the cannon's fuse was lit. The wadded parachute spewed out in a cloud of sparks and smoke. The force of being yanked from my perch in the balloon nearly broke my neck."

She bit her lip, clutched her chin in her hand, amazed and a little amused. "But you landed all right. Obviously, you're still alive."

"I got down, smiled bravely and bowed to the crowd, then I went off and got very sick. Vowed then and there that stunts didn't have to be part of the flying I wanted to do."

She could see the sense of that. Ordinary flying such as he wanted to do was dangerous enough.

Tom took her to another airshow following the one at Hutchinson. A large show to demonstrate the capabilities of aircraft, rather than stunt-flying. He introduced her to people he knew, Curtiss, Longren, Janickke, Cessna—all interested in the birth of aviation in Kansas and the difference it was going to make in people's lives. An interest she was beginning to strongly share.

Chapter Eleven

It wasn't the 4th of July, so the morning Lucy Ann heard sounds outside her house like a string of popping firecrackers, she knew that her friends had arrived in the Symington's motorcar to pick her up. She tied on her bonnet, peeked into the mirror over the halltree, and grabbed her things: suffragette badge, banner, and box of handouts.

Meg was coming up the path when she stepped onto the porch and closed the door behind her. "Aurelia doesn't want to shut off the motor and have to crank it up again so she sent me to get you."

Out at the road past the picket fence, Aurelia sat hunched over the wheel of her and Owen's noisy, shimmying, shuddering black Model T Ford like she was holding a charging monster. She motioned for the other two to hurry.

"All ready?" she asked after Lucy Ann climbed into the slick backseat and Meg got in front. They assured her they were all set to go. The motorcar lurched with a pop and a bang and they hurtled down the road reaching an incredible twenty miles an hour. As they passed Tom Reilly's farm, Aurelia peered through the isinglass window toward his barn and shouted over the auto's noise, "That man still trying to build a fool flying machine?"

Lucy Ann answered more quietly that he was.

Meg shrugged and commented, "I know most people don't agree but I think man is going to fly, with the right apparatus and know-how."

Aurelia hurrumphed, "Well, that man's a radical, and dangerous to be around if you ask me."

"Heavens, Aurelia," Lucy Ann said in a near-shout before she could catch herself, "Tom Reilly is no more a danger than your Owen. Or—or Hamilton. Tom is an inventor, he has different ideas about how to improve life for folks. He doesn't just look at today, he looks at tomorrow—far into the future. He's—adventurous."

In the front seat, Aurelia and Meg exchanged glances. The car zig-zagged past a hole in the road and nearly went into the ditch before Aurelia regained control.

She gripped the wheel and came straight to the point, shouting over the engine racket, "We don't think you should spend so much time with Mr. Reilly, Lucy Ann." Her head bobbed agreement to her own words. "We care about you. You know that we do. Don't we, Meg?"

"We don't want you to get hurt," Meg agreed.

"I'm doing fine and I hardly see Tom at all anymore, you all keep me so busy!"

After accompanying Tom to the airshows, she had been invited by her family and friends to almost daily quilting parties, afternoon "teas," and suffragette marches.

She was asked to help out with money-raisers for the suffrage campaign-fund by selling doughnuts and sandwiches. She served at money-raising dinners and ice cream socials 'til she felt run ragged.

They were all good causes and she wanted to do her part. But she was aware that involving her was also a means to keep her away from Tom Reilly. Did her friends, her own daughter, Rachel, and her sister-in-law Selinda, have any idea how paper-thin their ploy to 'take care of her' was?

"Where to today?" she asked now, changing the subject.

"Ness City," Aurelia shouted over her shoulder. "Dodge

City day-after-tomorrow."

"Will the other women be there?"

"As large a group as we could inform about the march."

For weeks, they had taken sojourns to neighboring towns where they spoke on the street corners, gathered petition signatures to give women the vote, and handed out little reminders that stated, "Give the women a Square Deal."

As much as she agreed—she wanted the vote as much as any of them—it was hard to be gone and still keep up work on her farm. And she told the truth when she said she saw little of Tom. He'd likely have another aeroplane completed before she ever got to see him again.

A few days after the trips to Ness City and Dodge with Aurelia and Meg, Selinda and Rachel insisted Lucy Ann accompany them to hear Sylvia Parkhurst, English suffragette, speak in Topeka. Although she was tired of being out and about so much and had been thinking of inviting Tom to supper, Lucy Ann instead agreed to the trip to Topeka to hear Miss Parkhurst. She sat back in the large meeting hall with the other women to listen.

Miss Parkhurst, a handsome woman in a dark suit and in command at the podium, began by quoting, " 'If the weakness of our Constitutions, if opinion and manners did not forbid us to march to glory by the same paths as the Men, we should at least equal and sometimes surpass them in our love for the public good.' "

"Those," she told them, beginning to pace the stage, "are the sentiments of an American woman spoken in Philadelphia in 1780. One hundred thirty years have passed and we women still cannot *vote* for *the public good!*"

At the minutes ticked on, Lucy Ann found herself impassioned, listening to Miss Parkhurst. She had no arguments with the Englishwoman, with her sentiments.

Suffrage *was* the keystone of all women's rights. Women had been held down and discriminated against for far too long. Yes, back in 'eighty-seven they were awarded the right to vote in school and municipal affairs, but it was wrong to continue to deny women the vote on state and national matters.

Equally with men, women deserved the right, the power, to make or change laws through the vote. From emancipation of women would flow a source of good for all humanity. They must make *male* legislators listen, women must have equal justice.

In the next weeks, Lucy Ann joined her women-friends in the cause with more zeal. Later that spring, when the suffrage amendment was submitted to the legislature, the women's movement was able to provide over one hundred supporting petitions signed by some 25,000 Kansas men and women. Under such lobbying pressure the measure passed the House and Senate. But it was only a beginning. It would be up to voters in next year's elections to ratify the measure.

Selinda held a supper to celebrate the early win for women's cause and to welcome Leonard home.

He had initiated and helped pass other interesting reforms: a workman's compensation law, a Blue Sky law providing for state inspection of all stocks sold in Kansas, a first time provision for registration of births and deaths. Money was appropriated for a new insane asylum. And October 12, Columbus Day, would be a public holiday in the future.

As the families sat around the dinner table, he quoted Representative J. A. Mahurin from Coffey County concerning suffrage, "I'm proud to cast a vote to enthrone the fair women of Kansas on that pedestal of equal rights for which they have battled so long and for which they are so eminently fitted to adorn and occupy."

Everyone laughed. Emmaline lifted her coffee cup and said with a wry smile, "Hear! Hear! Here's to Kansas, the first state in the Union to consider woman suffrage back in 1859. Here's to all those Kansas women for never giving up no matter how many times they've been denied the vote. However flowery Representative Mahurin may speak, don't we all agree with him?"

There was a chorus of *yesss*, the chink of cups meeting. Rachel spoke up, her eyes glossy with excitement, her chin high. "I haven't always agreed with the way David has voted in elections. I can hardly wait to vote my own say."

"We have to work hard," Selinda warned, "if the measure is to be ratified. We can't let the public forget for a moment that women deserve full and equal voting rights."

Lucy Ann agreed, "It's time justice was ours." If she spoke not only about the women's vote but included as well the right to do as she pleased, personally, no one seemed to notice.

Early summer was the busiest time on the farm. Lucy Ann engaged Lucas to help her out, and, ignoring her family's wishes otherwise, attended several aviation shows with Tom. In May, there was the demonstration of Glenn Curtiss aeroplanes at Walnut Grove in Wichita. In June, an aviation meet at Salina, and so on.

It was hard to remember, sometimes, that she no longer had to be frugal. That she could hire Lucas Davis to do her farmwork in her place as often and for as long as she liked, and pay him as generously as she pleased.

On a couple of occasions Selinda had politely and pri-

115

vately asked after her plans for her money, had she made up her mind yet? She could only say that when she knew herself what those plans might be, others would know, too.

As far as she could tell, both Leonard and Selinda continued to keep her secret.

Although she and Tom had never witnessed a casualty at the meets, she knew the possibility existed. One thing that bothered her about the aerial shows was the thirst for blood exhibited by some of the spectators. From overheard comments she knew some folks came expecting to see a terrifying death from the skies. Even hoped to see such a thing.

And aviation, so new and so much of it untried, was dangerous.

"Someone has to make the sacrifice," Tom said. "There are no directions, no rules. The air shows are fun for some, they enjoy the 'death-defying' aspects. For others, like me, the meets are a place to ask questions, witness tests, compare aeroplanes. Learn for the future, a good, safe future."

He seemed to enjoy having her along, and she found her own interest in the design and construction of aeroplanes growing and nearly equal to his.

If the aeroplane he presently planned, a "tractor type" monoplane with the propeller in front wasn't the answer to flying, the next one would be.

He had long liked the simplicity of the Bleriot design. Louis Bleriot, in July 1909, crossed the English Channel by air, in a cleanly designed monoplane. That craft had fewer guy wires and struts than most, which enhanced its speed. An aircraft, Tom explained to her, had better be a lot faster than autos or trains or why build it?

At a meet in late June, they met Roland Garros, who flew a Bleriot monoplane. Tom was excited to learn from

Garros that it was possible to buy a kit, a copy of the Bleriot, from the Queen Aeroplane Company in New York City.

As they headed for their train for the trip home, Tom told her, "Along with my own plans, I want to borrow the best ideas from others to build my own aeroplane. From a scientific and business perspective, I believe I must know all there is to learn. I wonder if the Queen Aeroplane Company would allow me to visit, learn all I can from them?"

She stopped, adjusted her hat flopping in the warm wind and asked, "Why just visit? Maybe they will give you work for a time, work you can learn by. You could write them a letter and ask."

"Fine idea, Lucy Ann!" He leaned down and lightly kissed her forehead. Then taking her arm, he guided them toward the train depot further down the street. She was left wondering what had just happened, then realized the light touch of his lips on her forehead was a simple thank you, nothing more.

She was in the garden, pulling beets for pickling, when Tom rode over to show her an answer that had come to his letter. They went to sit on her back step and he told her, "The Queen Aeroplane Company has agreed to let me work on the assembly line for one month to learn all I can. While I'm there, I'm going to test fly with their more experienced pilots."

"When do you leave?" She smiled her congratulations, wiped the dirt from her hands on her apron, then touched a cleaner part of her apron to her perspiring face.

"Right away. Will you mind watching after my place as well as yours while I'm gone? Joey and his pa will do the actual work—"

She laid a hand on his arm. "Of course I don't mind. I'm excited for you, Tom. It'll just put you that much further down the road to your dream. I wish you godspeed and good luck. I'll be anxious to hear from you when you return."

While he was away, Selinda and Rachel spirited her off to Topeka to hear President of the United States, William Howard Taft speak. She was not as reluctant to accompany them as the younger women seemed to think. She was almost positive women would win the vote in national affairs soon, and she wanted to be as well informed as possible.

Of course, Leonard, one of a group of progressive spokesmen that included other newspaper editors—William Allen White, Henry Allen, and Joseph L. Bristow—wanted Theodore Roosevelt for the next President. Roosevelt had shown himself well in his previous run as president, and in the war with Cuba.

She respected and admired Leonard for his leanings. Rachel's husband, David, was also a Roosevelt man. But as future voters, she and the other women planned to know as many sides as possible. In the end they would follow their own minds.

Taft was a giant of a fellow, over six feet tall and weighing over three hundred pounds. His manner was gentle, friendly. She listened carefully to him expound on what he wanted for the American people. As popular as he had been in Kansas when first elected, it sounded to her as though he was betraying progressive policies as some claimed. He was backing down to the bray of standpatters. Maybe he should have stayed a judge, a job which some said he loved far more than he liked being president. He called the White House the "loneliest place on earth."

She wouldn't make up her mind just yet, but in the end she would probably side with Leonard on Roosevelt for her choice. She was in favor of many of the progressive platforms Roosevelt supported. Among others, direct senatorial elections, the short ballot, primaries, *woman suffrage,* minimum wage laws, industrial minimum wage, industrial compensation, and the abolition of child labor.

As she sat abstractedly listening to the President of the United States speak, it came to her that she had led three different lives, almost as three different people. First as a young German-American farm girl, innocence ruined and her life nearly lost at the hands of savage Sioux Indians. A second, decently good life as wife to Admire and raising Leonard, and Rachel. And now she led a third life of—besides owning her own farm—politics, and aeroplanes, and much that was exciting and new. Thanks to changes in herself, thanks to Tom, and thanks to a changing world. It was invigorating to be alive, hard to believe that she had once been very sure she would kill herself.

Tom returned from his month in New York filled with enthusiasm; he could hardly wait to begin building his new aircraft. He showed her his plans on paper, opened crates of parts he brought home with him as though it were Christmas in August.

Slowly, under his skilled hands, the aircraft began to take shape in his barn. His aeroplane would be a two-place, Bleriot-like monoplane with forward propeller, a six-cylinder radial motor, light steel-tubing frame, enlarged gas tank and enclosed body and wings. A super-fine flying machine!

In the next weeks, he slaved over the construction night and day. More confident now, the work moved steadily and with few hitches. She was sure, in his excitement, that if she didn't take him a meal now and then that he would forget to eat. Occasionally she tried to draw him out about other matters around his farm that needed attention. Like the pesky rabbits.

"Jack rabbits are eating up your farm, Tom. Have you noticed?" She stood by in his machine-littered barn with a cloth-covered plate. He was working at a table with the spokey-looking engine he had brought back. When he didn't answer, she spoke more forcefully, "I never saw so many rabbits in all my time! Joey can't get rid of them even though he's earning seven cents for every rabbit-skin. They keep multiplying, thick as flies on a—" *cowpie*, she finished silently, catching herself just in time from an unseemly remark. Tom probably wouldn't have heard, anyway.

"Huh?" He turned away from the engine he tinkered with and accepted the plate of food. He stepped into a puddle of sunshine slanting through the small window and motioned for her to take a seat on one of the large crates. He sat down on a crate across from her.

"I don't have time to battle rabbits," he told her, digging into the plate of meat loaf and roast potatoes. He quirked a grin at her. "Glad you brought meat loaf. A neighbor of my Mount Hope Grandpa told me one time that he had eaten so much rabbit meat in his day that he could throw one ear forward and the other back."

She laughed with him, picturing the foolishness.

When he had finished the food he handed her the plate and fork, wiped his mouth, and asked, "You about ready to name my aircraft? It's not finished, yet," he waved a hand at the large aeroplane skeleton glimmering in the shadows of the barn, "but does it have to wait til it's finished for a name?"

She hesitated, plate and dish towel in hand. She felt nervous as she looked at him. She wasn't very good at this sort of thing. Selinda, or Emmaline, who were writers, might be more creative. But finally she told him, "I did think of a name. At first I thought of Prairie bird, other names like that. Then, I wanted to name your aircraft for here, for the place it was built. What do you think of The Paragon Spirit?"

He nodded, clapped his palms together. His face held a big grin as he crossed to her, so close she thought for a minute he was going to put his arms around her, hug her. When he didn't, she felt the faintest disappointment. He said, "Lucy Ann, that name is perfect. And the next plane we can call Spirit II, and so on."

She was glad that he was pleased. Her heart thumped at his closeness and she stepped back. She stood sidewise to him, studied him over her shoulder. Dust motes filtered through the slanted sunshine between them. *And so on,* he had said. "You are going to build others, then? A line of them?"

He went back to sit down. "Each one better than the one before. Until I've learned everything I can. I want to show people, business folk, what an aeroplane can do, and interest them in having their own. Then, I want to build and sell aeroplanes. And the name Paragon Spirit is perfect, just perfect."

It was next spring before the Paragon Spirit was ready. Just as Tom was putting on the finishing touches, W. J. "Pigeon" Nelson's wild west show came to town.

A thicket of wagons and buggies, a stagecoach, numerous tents, and fifty or so colorfully dressed characters created a small village of their own at the fairgrounds west of town. Such shows brought life to the community, and even a little extra trade. Tom made arrangements with Pigeon to allow him to exhibit and fly the newly completed

Paragon Spirit at the end of the show. It would be a demonstration of how far society had progressed since the old pioneering days.

Seated with the rest of the crowd at the edge of the dusty arena through the warm spring afternoon, Lucy Ann enjoyed the rodeo stunts, trick roping and riding and the staged, noisy, stagecoach robbery. She found the fake Indian raids, scalpings and killings ludicrous and distasteful in the extreme. She was left shaking with old fear and anger and was relieved when they were over.

There were some things folks needed no reminders of, wanted to just forget.

Anyhow, the show was not why she had come. She was far more interested to see the first real flight of the Paragon Spirit.

It was time for the aviation demonstration after which Tom was scheduled to say a few words about the new phenomena.

As the engine revved, the sleek silver Spirit hardly vibrated. The engine hummed. Tom, at the controls, looked in command, and excited. Lucy Ann stood back with the others, watching the aircraft roll away across the field at a speed surely seventy-five miles an hour. Then the Spirit lifted into the blue as easily as a bird.

"Don't hardly seem possible a body could do that," a farmer spoke in awe, off her right shoulder, "fly thataway."

With necks craned, the crowd watched. The Spirit soared higher and higher toward a few puffy clouds. Another man near Lucy Ann spoke, "That man can go anywhere he wants and not be bothered by bad roads or scary horses or a damned balky automobile. Now that's somethin'!"

"Yes," Lucy Ann said, as much to herself as answering the speaker, "it is."

Chapter Twelve

Tom was not a show-off flyer, but his flying forty-odd miles
that day, almost as far northeast as Great Bend, at an alti-
tude of 4,000 feet, impressed even the most serious
doubters at the event and those who only heard about it,
later, when it became the talk of the county.

Pigeon Nelson's Wild West Show was one thing, the
hotel supper in Topeka that Selinda and Leonard took Lucy
Ann to a short time later was quite another for her.

Many of Kansas's most important folks were there and
after the supper they would hear Victor Herbert, famous
conductor and composer, in concert. His songs, "Ah, Sweet
Mystery of Life," and "I'm Falling in Love with Someone"
from his operetta, *Naughty Marietta*, were quite the rage.

At the elegant supper, Lucy Ann carefully studied which
fork she should use for the roast duck, and also privately re-
flected that her best clothes of the past were no longer suit-
able. Sneaking a look at the beautifully gowned women
around her, she made a mental note to have some new
dresses made. Heaven knew she could afford it.

She should be thankful she supposed, that a pleasant
side-effect to Selinda's continued efforts to draw her away
from associating with Tom, was that she was subjected to
more of the finer things of life. Not that she was always
comfortable in gatherings such as tonight's. She rarely was.
But she enjoyed sitting back, unobserved, while she
watched others and listened to them.

If they knew her, knew what happened to her as a girl,

123

she might not have been welcome in their fine, respectable circle. But most folks only knew that she was Representative Voss's sister, that the two of them had grown up in Western Kansas and still lived there in a place called Paragon Springs.

Nor did she feel she was at the affair under false pretenses. She felt rather, that many folks didn't always understand the true complexion of happenings to other people. Her own parents, had they not been killed, would have seen her as *ruined*. Most folks felt that way at that time. It had taken her years to see that the outrage wasn't her fault and that she was still Lucy Ann. A nice human being, not garbage. Still, she might never fit in, completely, with high society.

Leonard was different. She liked to see how comfortable he was with those she considered 'his people'. Many of his friends were famous all over the world. William Allen White down the table, editor of the *Emporia Gazette*, was at the moment talking with Leonard. Probably talking politics. Like Leonard, White, a short man with thinning hair and a friendly face, was a Roosevelt man, and it was clear they were in amiable, though animated, agreement. Any more agreement and they would nod their heads off, she thought with a smile.

After the supper, as folks noisily gathered in the hotel foyer to wait for their phaetons to take them to the concert, Lucy Ann escaped to the edge of the crowd for a minute's quiet peace. She found a grouping of chairs against the wall and took one. Selinda came to ask if she needed anything.

"Just resting, but thank you, dear. Would you like to sit down?"

"I just heard the most unsettling thing," Selinda said, slipping gracefully into a damask chair beside her. "I was talking with the president of the state historical society, and he tells me that in the past fifty years, twenty-four hundred towns have disappeared from the Kansas map! Can you believe that? Thousands of towns that started up with hopes and dreams no longer exist. Puff. Gone." She waved her hands.

"I can believe it," Lucy Ann said, recalling the long years of struggle for Paragon Springs. It was truly a miracle that they had managed to hang on, keep the town alive as long as they had, if sometimes only barely. Paragon Springs so easily could have been one of the statistics, one of the twenty-four hundred towns that vanished "off the map."

Later, during the ride across town with Leonard and Selinda, then at the Herbert concert, and for days afterward, she couldn't stop thinking about the lost towns.

She knew, finally, what she was going to do with her money to help the town. The idea had actually skirted the edges of her mind for some time, she realized. But with everyone so against her association with Tom, she had been almost afraid to think it. Now she had her plan, a clear decision.

When Tom got his aircraft perfected to the point he was satisfied, she was going to give him money to start an aeroplane factory at Paragon Springs. She had become a believer. She wanted to be part of his dream, of building and selling aeroplanes as a commerce; aeroplanes for the whole country's use, for improved lives. She felt certain there could be no better way to guarantee the town's future for the next hundred and more years.

She just hoped her friends and family would agree with her opinion, when the time came to tell them. Most still believed that aviation was an idiot's pipedream, with no future except as entertainment in reckless barnstorming stunts.

For now, proof otherwise would be hard to establish, but it would come.

That year that followed, 1912, was the busiest in Lucy Ann's memory. As often as possible, she traveled with the other women from Paragon Springs to campaign for the final vote for suffrage.

By horse-drawn rigs, sometimes in mounted groups on horseback, and a few times by chugging auto-caravan, they joined every parade, every gathering and event within traveling distance where they might demonstrate their cause, and hand out pamphlets. All eyes of the country were on Kansas women to see if they could succeed getting the vote. They would not fail, this time.

Several of the little towns they visited were squalid, dusty villages with flies swarming over everything. The women who came out to see them looked haggard and worn, their children sickly.

Such as that would change when women were voted into office, when women got the vote, Lucy Ann determined. She hated filth. There had been one instance when both Rachel, and Meg, got deathly ill from drinking contaminated well water. Before they recovered everyone worried that they might have contacted typhoid. It was a close call. Causing more than one comment that what the Kansas country needed was a good clean-up. She would like a good strong hand in such a campaign.

Tom was building his second monoplane that summer. It would be sleeker and faster. He believed as Clyde Cessna did, "Speed is the only reason for flying." Fortunately, speed was much safer in the air than on land. Time and again in Cessna's flights, he was proving that he could fly a mile a minute, and more, in all kinds of weather. Still, he was considered one of the "flying madmen," by the business folk he talked to in Wichita, in Topeka. No one could see the aeroplane for other than entertainment, aerobatics. Certainly not as part of business.

"They have to be shown and shown again," Tom told her. So he, too, was busy, performing at least two flights a month at shows all around Kansas. Nowadays, he did not take his aeroplane by haywagon, he *flew* to his destination. He asked her to fly with him, in his two-seater, but she couldn't quite summon the nerve. Someday, she would. In between trips, he worked on the second Paragon Spirit he was building.

Two events that would forever make a difference in her life happened that fall. First, the woman suffrage amendment carried in the November elections, and Kansas became the eighth state to give women full suffrage, the right to vote in coming state and national affairs.

All over Kansas, women celebrated the win of a long, long battle. Across the rest of the nation, other women celebrated for them, and for Oregon and Arizona who also gave women the vote that year.

Then, at Christmastime, Leonard announced first to his family, then to his friends, and finally in his newspaper, that in the year, 1914, two years hence, he would be a candidate for the office of Governor of Kansas.

Just last month, his favored candidate for President of the United States, Theodore Roosevelt, had lost to Woodrow Wilson. The loss was blamed on the general weakening of the Republican Party by a split—the old guard standpatters versus the new progressives. The 1912 Kansas legislature was largely Democratic this time, Leonard was

127

one of the few Republican representatives still in office. He was seeking additional ways to benefit his state in the future.

Social betterment would be his platform. Chiefly he wanted to see improved health practices implemented, more hospitals built, and he wanted to bring an end to fake medicine distribution. Equally he meant to see that child labor laws were obeyed. The laws were there but were too often skirted for unsound reasons, padding the money-belt of the employers who would have to pay adults higher wages. There had to be an end to using children under the age of twelve as slaves, working fourteen-hour days for next to nothing.

She was as thrilled, as proud, as she would ever be, thinking that the day was near at hand when she would be marking a ballot for her own brother for Governor. And in the process making a mark for better lives for her fellow Kansans of every age.

Other newspapers picked up Leonard's announcement and in no time the news that he meant to run for governor was common knowledge around the state.

During a rare period when both Lucy Ann and Tom were at home on their farms, he rode over to congratulate her on her "famous brother." She asked him about his political leanings.

"I'm not much of a political person," he said, "although I try to know what's going on and I do vote in most elections." He waited for her to join him at her kitchen table before digging into the warm apricot pie she had served him. "At times it's hard to tell which varmint in that cage we call the capitol might be less of a rat than the others. Or maybe they are all rats, they tell lies so much."

He looked suddenly embarrassed, and he put his fork

down. "I'm not talking about your brother. I like Leonard. I think he is honest, a square-dealer, who really cares about folks, all folks. One of these days, maybe I'll get more interested in how the country is run. I'll offer aid where I'm needed, help obtain the vote for causes I believe in. Right now the aeroplane business takes my time."

A silence followed, and then she told him, smiling, waggling her fork in her lifted hand, "I read in the *Echo* about Phil Billard's latest flight."

Their friend, Phil, was the son of Topeka mayor, J. B. Billard. Phil had recently flown his Longren pusher aeroplane in loops and circles and figure-eights around the statehouse dome. It was only a sixteen minute flight, but it had brought out the natives in huge numbers to watch the "free show."

Tom chuckled. "I heard about it. I guess J.B. isn't too happy about his son flying over the city. J.B. arrived in Topeka fifty years ago by covered wagon and he still thinks that's the best way to travel."

He held up his cup. "If you don't mind, I'll have one more cup of your fine coffee, maybe a smidgen more of pie, then I have to go. You know, the work never stops."

She still hadn't told him her plans for an aeroplane manufactory to salvage Paragon Springs's future. But she felt the time to tell him was near. His aeroplanes would only improve. And mankind around the world would grow wiser to their use, and benefit.

Looking ahead to the elections of 1913 when she would be actually voting, Lucy Ann began to follow political debates in the newspapers more faithfully. It seemed doubly important to do so now, too, that Leonard had announced he meant to run for governor. She agreed with most policies of the Progressive Republican party. But at the moment she could find little fault with Kansas's Democratic Governor Hodges's platforms. She wondered if he might run for re-election.

Hodges rightly insisted that Kansas needed more business and less politics. He wanted more industrial and agricultural development of the state. Of course he was right in that they must build permanent roads. From all accounts, the auto was there to stay, a part of nearly every life. He also wanted water storage reservoirs and heaven knew that would help Kansas's water problems.

As a farmer and citizen, she would enjoy voting come election time.

She had just finished her spring plowing in March when she joined Tom to see an exhibition performed by their friend, Clyde Cessna at Kingman, west of Wichita. Clyde was a Kingman County farmer, as well as an aviator, so she enjoyed visiting with him on a double score, although they talked aeroplanes more than crops. Clyde was considered a genius by many. He made even the bolts that held his machines together. His wife, Europa, sewed fabric for his aircraft. His monoplanes were clean, fast, and efficient. He meant his expensive aeroplanes to pay off, and not just by performing "fool-killer" stunt flights. He believed as Tom and she did, that the time was near at hand for standard production and paying customers and Kansas was as good a place as any for a commercial aviation industry to set its course.

Back home, a couple of days later, she was prepared to discuss that very matter with Tom when Selinda begged her ride to Topeka with her on the train and she agreed. The legislature would be adjourning, they could join Leonard and have a few days in the city with him, shopping, seeing plays, visiting acquaintances, before returning home with him.

At their first meal together in Topeka, Leonard seemed abnormally quiet, maybe a little worn down. He seemed only to want to hear about things from home, wanted her and Selinda to do most of the talking while he listened. When she asked if he was feeling well he smiled and said he was fine.

After supper, at a Maude Adams performance of *Peter Pan* at Topeka's Grand Theater, he seemed to have his mind elsewhere and showed only minor interest in the colorful, noisy activity on the stage. Lucy Ann eyed him worriedly in the darkened theater, then decided that *Peter Pan* was not for everyone, after all. He was an adult, and weary from an arduous legislative session. Women and children in the audience seemed to be enjoying the play the most.

Still, concern for Leonard nagged at her. The feeling was revived during intermission when they joined the rest of the audience in the theater lobby for refreshment.

People they knew from many previous such occasions, who normally greeted Leonard, Selinda, and her with warmth and friendliness, behaved oddly toward them. She couldn't fault Leonard's friends for their manners, they were polite enough, but conversations were strained. There was a mystery in the air, and no clues. The three of them were being treated almost as strangers, quite different from ever before.

Chapter Thirteen

Intermission was almost over when a man broke from the crowd and rushed over to the three of them with a wide smile.

"Philander, how are you?" Leonard's smile was tired but friendly. He shook the man's hand and introduced him to Selinda and Lucy Ann. Lucy Ann hadn't personally met him before, but she had heard of him, had seen him at gatherings before.

Philander Winslow was probably the least popular human being in the building. He was a wealthy, influential Kansas City mill owner. Winslow had been born in the south, into a family who had been the embodiment of southern aristocracy "befo the wah," as he put it. He was slight of build, about fifty, unmarried. He deliberately spoiled the several women who lived with him: his mother, grandmother, sister, and two aunts. The women in his life seemed to dote on him, possibly because he fulfilled their every whim.

None of that, though, was the reason Lucy Ann didn't like him very much. A legislator, himself, from a northeast district, he had fought to halt last year's bill to abolish child labor. She remembered him saying at a party, "But of course we have to work children if there aren't enough niggers! Grown white folks expect more than a man can afford to pay. How is a man to make a profit, if he can't have children working for him? And children *want* to help 'put the bacon on the family tables' so to speak."

What he really meant, most believed, was that he wanted

no obstacle to the considerable riches it took to buy expensive baubles, and to pay for travel abroad, for his lazy, helpless, southern women.

Lucy Ann was glad the measure to abolish child labor had passed in spite of his efforts to kill it. His claim that the children who worked for him weren't abused, that he "cared for the children in his garment mills just as kindly as his family had always looked after their slaves in the past," was hogwash. Investigation had proved otherwise.

Philander had a penchant for gossip. He liked attention, any kind of attention, and maybe that was behind his habit of pushing himself excessively on other people anywhere he could capture them. There was a rumor that he also had his eye on the governorship, in competition with Leonard.

She doubted that he would be taken seriously. At one time or another he had been a member of three different parties, Republican, Democrat, and Socialist. He hopped about like a political flea, as though unsure what he stood for except where it benefitted him personally.

She drew in a slow breath, cautioning herself to hold her tongue, as he now turned to her. He swung his massive gold-headed cane, bowed slightly, showing the knife-sharp part in his wavy hair. His eyes, when they found hers, seemed to share a secret that delighted him. "Isn't Maude Adams a grand performer?" he asked, taking her hand in his and squeezing. "Isn't the play just a charm?"

She was puzzled at the comment, because he didn't seem to be talking about the play. She told him, "Yes, Maude is a fine actress. We're enjoying the play very much, thank you." She pulled her hand from his and did her best to smile. Leonard and Selinda were moving away. "Excuse me, please, Mr. Winslow." She didn't want to be rude, then saw that he had already turned to gush over someone else, swinging the gold-headed cane and bowing.

When they were back in the darkened theater for the second act she couldn't rid her mind of the strangeness of the evening. Maybe the stand-offishness shown Leonard and his family by the others had to do somehow with partisan politics. There might have been strong disagreement with Leonard over some measure these past three months.

Or the explanation could be that most of Leonard's friends in the legislature were worn out from three months of wrestling with difficult bills and laws at the statehouse. It was hard to say, but likely all the men wanted to return to their regular lives.

She probably worried needlessly, but she meant to keep her eyes and ears open. It didn't matter that Leonard was a grown man now, a wise and competent man, her concern was hard to stifle.

Lucas was as able a replacement for her as she could find, but at times when she was away, Lucy Ann missed work on the farm. She missed the farm in general, missed her fields, her animals, her house. She decided to put off, for a while yet, her plan to discuss with Tom her idea of an aviation factory. That plan, when she finally set it into motion, was going to consume a great deal of her time and attention.

Milo maize had been a good crop for her; she was ready to try others. This year she would try twenty acres of sugar cane, and twenty of kafir for sorghum. She had heard those crops would "knit" the soil and keep it from blowing away. Winds would always be a travail in Western Kansas, she supposed. Ideas for dealing with the wind were constantly discussed.

She thought the best use of wind, though, was going to

be aviation! Certainly, along with Tom's knowledge, the flat land and constant winds contributed to his ever more successful flights. Sometimes she went to watch his test flights. He begged her to go up with him, and see for herself what flying was like, but she still was not able to strike up the courage. Often he came over to her house with detailed reports.

Adding to their encouragement, his and other aviators' flights were being covered by serious journalists, by newspaper men and women who increasingly stressed the commercial advantages of flight in their stories. Lurid tales of derring-do appeared less frequently. In turn, the minds that controlled the business world, if not totally convinced, nevertheless were showing signs that they were gradually making an about-face.

Except for those rare instances, visits and watching the tests, and an excursion with Tom in July to see an exhibition of A. K. Longren flying his new tractor biplane, she worked steadily on the farm.

She loved being out in the open fields, in the sunshine and fresh air. Her aching back and sore muscles she saw as symbols of her accomplishments. Aches and pains and dirt could be mended with warm baths, retiring to bed an hour or two earlier. To start a new day, fresh. No matter whatever else might happen in her life, what other interests might capture her mind, she would hang on tightly as well to her ties to the farm.

The Sunday she walked into church and everyone turned to stare at her she at first attributed to the fact that she had neglected to attend church for several Sundays in a row. She nodded and smiled back sheepishly. Then, she knew that whatever was amiss had to do with a lot more than her failing to hear a few Sunday sermons. A chill crept over her.

She almost stumbled as she continued walking to her pew. In some of the faces she saw deep sympathy. Her close friends, Meg, Aurelia, Bethany Hessler, her own family—Rachel and David—and others, looked mortified enough to weep for her. What made her go numb was the shock, and even revulsion, directed her way from the faces of others less well-known to her.

She sat through the service, hardly hearing a word. She sang old familiar hymns with the others, but wasn't sure she actually voiced the words. What had happened? What was wrong? She resisted the urge to get up and run out, go home.

She had looked for Leonard and Selinda. They weren't in attendance that Sunday but that wasn't unusual. As newspaper publishers and editors, they often visited other churches in order to fairly cover all county churches in write-ups for their religion pages.

After the closing prayer, she left the cooler shadows of the church interior for the hot bright sunshine outside. Waiting by the door, the preacher squeezed her hand with a pious look of pity in his eyes before he looked away to grasp the hand of the next parishioner.

In the churchyard, she walked about looking for Rachel and David, felt a wide empty circle of avoidance around her where normally folks would be asking how she was, how her crops fared, and so on. She remembered that while she was in Topeka with Leonard and Selinda, she had felt this same sort of rejection, as though she had a contagious disease.

Something was terribly wrong. As groups of folk formed to visit in the churchyard, covert glances were thrown her way. There were hushed whisperings; the caw of a crow in the tree by the church was very loud and eerie in comparison.

Rachel and David came rushing to her side and from the look on her daughter's face the world had ended. A deep frown creased David's face as he said, rather than asked, "You're coming home to Sunday dinner with us, Ma, come along."

"All right. Thank you for the *invitation*." She pulled back as Rachel clutched her arm and tried to hurry her toward their buggy faster than she wanted to walk. "Bless the skies, tell me what is going on here or I won't take another step!"

"No, Mama, not now," Rachel cried in a low voice. She looked close to tears, her face heated by more than the sun. "I'll tell you at home. I've invited some others. Let's just go, now, please."

David looked as distraught as Lucy Ann had ever seen him and she knew he wasn't going to tell her anything, now, either. She nodded. "All right, we can go. But I want an explanation as soon as we get there." Lucy Ann had ridden horseback to church and she went to get Taffy from the church shed. They tied the mare to the back of David's buggy.

Rachel kept her head down as she climbed up into the seat beside David, he sat like stone and stared straight ahead. Zachary had ridden home on his own mount; Marcus and Amy, chattering in happy childhood innocence, squeezed in on each side of Lucy Ann in the back seat of the buggy. As they rolled away into the road, she could feel stares like shotgun pellets boring into her from folks still on the church grounds.

When they got to Rachel and David's farm, Meg and Hamilton were already there. Aurelia and Owen arrived in their Model T Ford auto a minute later. Emmaline was with them.

Then came the Hesslers in their phaeton they normally used to transport hotel guests. It wasn't unusual for the group of old friends to get together for Sunday dinner, but something about this day truly alarmed her.

"After dinner, Mama," Rachel said when she whispered that she must know what was going on, that instant.

The women were mostly silent as they quickly set out the meal. Rachel had cooked most of it, but the others had brought covered dishes, too. They ate in odd silence, then the children were sent outside to play. The grownups gathered in a tight knot in the parlor. She wouldn't have been surprised if Rachel had drawn the blinds and locked the doors, the way they were all acting.

"What is it?" she asked. "What is this about?"

No one said anything. "Meg, you'll tell me."

"All right. It has to do with me, too. Lucy Ann, somehow it has come out that Leonard killed a man when he was a boy. His opponents for the governorship, especially a man named Philander Winslow, intend to use that against him. They plan to claim that he killed in 'cold blood' although we know he did what he did to save my life."

Hamilton said, "We know that if Leonard hadn't stepped in then to help Meg, she probably would have been returned to St. Louis and her good-for-nothing monster of a husband, in a box."

She nodded. "But how do you know about the talk, the plan to use what Leonard did, against him? I haven't heard anything." With a sudden sinking heart, she realized that for some weeks now, since returning from Topeka, she had lived like a mole in a hole on her farm, happily blind and deaf to the rest of the world.

"Our guess is that it started in the capitol a few weeks

ago," Hamilton told her, and she remembered the behavior of the other legislators in Topeka that night at the play. "It started out as mild talk. We thought the story would die. But Philander Winslow is using it to bolster his chances for the governorship against Leonard and he's adding as much fire to it as he can, to serve himself. It's his only chance."

Emmaline added, "Winslow is saying voters must take a closer look at Leonard and his *black heart*, his devious past, but facts are that *he*, Winslow, is the true scoundrel."

"Dear God!" Lucy Ann was astounded. Philander was a man almost as shallow as his immaculate shirt-front; she didn't think the disclosure of the story would help him much. But it could do Leonard a great deal of harm. Why, oh why, now?

Hamilton leaned forward in his chair, "We still think the stories would have just died, but E.C. Osborne here in Paragon Springs befriended Winslow in a bid for importance for himself. He twisted the truth in his little rag of a newspaper 'til you wouldn't have recognized it, he made the stories headline news. Other papers picked up and carried the stories. Now gossip is burning the telephone wires like wildfire."

Lucy Ann tried to say something but Meg beat her to the punch.

"I've had several people ask me about the stories on the street, and at church today, wanting to know if they were true," Meg said. "I've tried to explain, put an end to the gossip, but some folks seem to enjoy scandal and want to make as much of it as possible."

Lucy Ann burst out, "You said 'stories'." She looked around at all of them. "There is more?"

Aurelia's eyes filled with tears and she came to sit beside her and take her hand. Her face was stricken. "Dearest

Lucy Ann, it is also being told that you were at one time—you were r-ravished by savages. If we had known this would happen, we would have done anything to stop it—"

"We'll put a stop to the talk, yet!" Will Hessler insisted from across the room. Bethany, beside him on the sofa, added, "Ain't no sense in bringing all this up now."

Why, then? Why was it happening? She clung to the arm of the sofa. In so many eyes, if the killing Leonard was forced to commit wasn't enough to render him unfit to serve as governor, the fact that his sister had been "got to" by "dirty redskins" surely would. "That *is* all, isn't it?" She felt very sick, and embarrassed that her disgrace had to be discussed, even within the circle of her dearest friends.

"We're sorry, Lucy Ann, but they are also saying you are now shamelessly cavorting with a man who thinks he can fly," Emmaline said softly.

That made her angry. *Cavorting?* She was trying to save her town, that was all. Build them an industry that would sustain the town in the future. A cold sensation settled in the pit of her stomach as she thought of something else. If they ever attacked Rachel—! Aurelia read her face and she didn't have to put it into words.

"So far," Aurelia said softly, squeezing her hand, "the perpetrators of this nastiness don't seem aware there was a-a baby."

Rachel, standing near the window next to David, turned her face into his chest, saying nothing. He led her toward the door and they went outside.

Lucy Ann sat stone-cold, and very, very angry. How dare they use the Indians' brutal assault on her person to say that Leonard wasn't fit for office? How dare they turn it around that his saving a life was cold-blooded murder? It wasn't fair, it wasn't true, it wasn't right. She was eternally grateful, though, that Ad had been dark-skinned, like Rachel, and most folks assumed that he was her father. Thank God they hadn't connected her beloved child with the awfulness of that attack on her body, on her soul.

"What can we do, Lucy Ann?" Owen was asking. "You know we will do anything for you and Leonard that we can. We'll stop this, somehow."

She nodded. "Thank you." They were the dearest friends in the world, always had been to her. Not one of them would have passed on the story of the outrage against her, of that she was confident. A few folks knew her and Leonard's true history, although it wasn't openly talked about. Even Admire might have said something some time long ago when he was drunk and upset, although a word of it wouldn't have been uttered sober. Somebody could have heard, passed the ugly story on. Things happened that way, as often as not, and she didn't blame Admire, either.

It wasn't important how the stories were revealed to be used against Leonard. It only mattered that something be done about them.

"Thank you all for standing by me and by Leonard," she said a short while later. "I want to think about this at home, alone, for a while." She went outside to join her children. She put her arm around Rachel. "It's going to be all right, Rachel, it really is going to be all right."

Rachel turned and her eyes were full of tears. "It's not fair what they are saying about you, Mama, not fair at all. Not fair what they are saying about Uncle Leonard being a killer—" Behind Rachel's tears, Lucy Ann saw a lot of her own anger and frustration, but not an inkling of self-pity. *Good.* Anger would sustain Rachel a lot better in what could be terrible times ahead. She kissed her cheek. Even managed a smile.

"No, it isn't fair, dearest. But quite a bit in life isn't fair. We won't let this best us, though. We are going to be fine, you'll see." She tried to sound more sure than she felt. "I want to go home, now, though. I have to have time to think."

David stepped forward, tossing aside the blade of grass he had been chewing. "I'll drive you home."

"No, but thank you. I want you to stay with Rachel. I'd like the long ride home on Taffy. It'll help me think, and Lord knows I need to think long and hard about this."

Chapter Fourteen

For a few days she stayed in her house, in a deep study, trying to decide what to do. She left the house only to do the most necessary chores.

Leonard came. The sight of her brother, such a decent person so unfairly damnified, nearly shattered her. With so little else to hold against him, his competition would be all-fired to use whatever they could.

They talked quietly for a long time. Without putting it in so many words they both realized that the killing of the bounty hunter, Frank Finch, might be explained and accepted by others as necessary. What would be harder to forgive would be her having been despoiled by Indians, and daring to walk among them as though it never happened.

"I'm so sorry, Lucy Ann. Likely none of this would have come out if I hadn't been running for office."

"Don't apologize to me, Leonard Voss!" She rose from her chair and paced. "You are one of the finest men who ever lived. Anyone who knows you, knows that." She faced him, and her voice quivered, "You would never hurt a fly, you have always cared about other people twice what you care about yourself. Damn these vicious gossip mongers! You have been good for Kansas as a representative in the legislature, you can do so much more as governor. Damn them if they try to stop you!"

He told her with a wry grin, "I've never heard you swear before."

"Swearing won't hurt the reputation I've got," she quipped back, "so I might as well say what I feel."

A few days after Leonard's visit, Tom came. She was embarrassed but had to face him sometime. He would have read all about her in the newspapers by now. She led the way to her small parlor where they stood looking at one another.

"I'm sorry, Lucy Ann." His voice was gentle, his face sympathetic. He came forward and took her hand.

He was so dear to her, he had been such a good friend these past few years. There had never been a really awkward moment between them, 'til now. It was hard to know what to do, to say. She squeezed his hand, then released it and went to sit in a chair on the other side of the room.

"I'm sorry, too, Tom, that you ever had to know about what happened to me." She spoke huskily, chin lifted but avoiding his eyes. "I suppose I'm as over that ugly, awful part of my life as much as I will ever be, but now the—the outrage suddenly seems to matter to other people." There was a harshness, an angry hurt in her voice that she couldn't soften.

"Doesn't matter to me, except I hate that you were hurt. You know that I am very fond of you, Lucy Ann—"

"Thank you. I hope that won't change, but if it does, I'll understand."

"How I feel about you won't ever change." His voice was full of feeling, honest affection. "You're still you, the Lucy Ann I've always known, whose company has meant so much to me."

His words warmed her heart, lifted some of the pain. He was saying, "I think you need to get away. There is an aviation meet soon, come with me." *Let me take you away from those who would hurt you,* his eyes insisted.

She gave him a grateful smile. "Thank you for asking,

thank you for your thoughtfulness. But I can't go with you, just now. I *am* going to go away for a while. I need to be by myself and have some time to think."

"I can take you!" he said, jumping to his feet, his voice warm with excitement and pleasure that he could do something for her. He flung out his arm. "I can fly you nearly to anywhere you want to go."

She laughed past the ache in her throat. "No, I have to go alone, Tom." And then, to feel that she was still clean, and all right to touch, she stood up and went to him, put her arms about him, just to feel him hug her back. He held her close, made a funny, affectionate sound in his throat. It was reassuring. As she pulled away, she reached up to graze his rough cheek with her fingertips and she smiled. "Thank you, Tom, for being you."

She had never told Rachel and David about the oil money. She went to tell them now, seeing it as a big chunk of good news to counteract the bad.

Once they recovered from their shock, they were put out with her for not telling them about it from the start.

"I had my reasons," she answered, "I still have them. Which brings me to the other reason I'm here. I am going to be away for a while and I wanted to let you know." She felt that Oklahoma, on Ad's land, was as good a place as any to think and she was overdue going down there, anyway.

"You can't go alone," Rachel caught her arms. "I'll go with you, Mama."

"Next time, maybe. This first time I want to go to Oklahoma by myself." She spoke firmly, so there would be no doubt about her wishes.

She concluded in those next few minutes that maybe her

children, at least, were realizing that she had a mind of her own. Anyway, they agreed.

Lucy Ann looked out the window of the Santa Fe train, silently marking how much the dusty plains of the Strip had changed from what she remembered. They rumbled through small towns, past enormous fields of golden wheat being threshed, past fields of broomcorn and kafir in the stack. Traveling along well-made roads were farm wagons loaded with grain, *automobiles* that looked like odd, tumbling-along black beetles. Rangelands were dotted with lean Texas longhorn cattle. Willows, cottonwoods, and elms lined the Salt Fork of the Arkansas River and the creeks.

What looked like a forest of windmills, as they neared Shelbyville, her destination, was her first sight of oil derricks.

Shelbyville had been boomed by an oil man from Pennsylvania named Shelby. What started as a boom-town of shacks and tents had been turned into a nice little town, surrounded by derricks, wheat fields and grazing lands.

"Black gold, liquid gold," they were calling oil. Admire's small claim, meant to be his part of a large cattle spread, had instead become enormously valuable because of black greasy liquid under the soil.

Although she hadn't seen Ad's friend, Lofty Gowdy, in years, they had written many letters back and forth. At first they wrote about Ad's death, then the land-lease, and finally the discovery of oil on the ranch. She spotted Lofty before he saw her as she stepped off the train at the Shelbyville station.

The first time she saw him back in 1873 he was a penniless, string-bean rider maybe eighteen or nineteen years old.

He was a lot the same, only twenty years older, at the time of the Run in 1893. Now he was grayhaired, his broad shoulders stooped a bit, and he had thickened around the middle although he was still very tall.

On the depot platform a big ginger-colored dog was jumping all over him and he was having trouble keeping the dog's big dusty paw prints off his fine suit. He swatted the dog away with his white hat, clamped the hat back on. In that moment he spotted her. For a moment he looked ready to cry for joy. "Lucy Ann! Hell if ain't you, prettier'n ever. Ad's Lucy Ann!"

"Hello, Lofty." They shook hands, he held hers like it might break off at the wrist if he wasn't tender with her. Ad's friends had always been that way. Most cowboys treated women as though they were very, very special, the delight of the world, regardless of who they were.

All at once she remembered that Lofty had hinted strongly in one of his letters after Ad's death that maybe the two of them should marry. Now, she felt her face warm a bit. She had pretended she didn't know what he was getting at back then and had continued writing as usual. That had happened so long ago he likely wouldn't remember it, she'd almost forgotten.

He had married someone else named Trudy, then she died, and he had married again, a woman named Opal. She asked now, after his family.

He took her bag in one hand, her elbow in the other and began to lead her down the street toward a black Model T Ford parked at the curb with the convertible top down. "Opal is fine, you can see she is making me fat with her good cooking. My children is scattered to hell and gone now they are almost grown. Daughter and her husband is in Houston, I got a son in Santa Fe, and one boy moved all the way to the Northwest, to Portland, Oregon. Distance don't mean nothin' now we got trains and automobiles."

"And aeroplanes, too. We'll be traveling by air before very long."

"Nah," he shook his head confidently. "I don't see that happenin'. That's just a foolish notion some folks got that'll die out one of these days."

I don't think so.

"Opal's sister took sick, sudden, and she's gone to take care of her down to Enid, but we'd still like for you to come stay at the house," he said as they reached his auto. She noticed that he limped, and she remembered that in one of his letters he had mentioned that he had fallen off of a derrick he was helping to build. He put her bag in the back of his auto, opened the side door and helped her in.

A little puff of wind blew up the street. Ahead of them, somebody honked their auto horn, and a team hitched to a wagon, frightened by the sudden noise, tried to pull away from the hitchrack before a man ran forward to calm them.

"I appreciate the invitation, Lofty, but I've come down here to do some thinking and I'd like to stay in town, at a hotel."

"Anything serious wrong up home?" He hesitated by the auto's open door with the crank in his hand and studied her face.

She waved him on out front to start the car and lied, with a smile, "No. Family matters. Some tittle-tattle, minor trouble, nothing bad." Not for the life of her would she tell the truth of her situation, even to a good, kind friend like Lofty.

After leaving her things in her room at the Morrison Hotel, they enjoyed refreshment downstairs in the dining room. She asked after others they both knew.

"Harlan Thorne has done real well up in Alaska, I hear tell," he told her. "When his friend, Knob, died, he took off for the north. Bama, when he got too old to ride, he went back to his folks in Alabama. Ain't sure where Flan Jones is now, ain't seen him in years. You probably know Jack Ambler is a banker in Guthrie. Got too old for horsebackin' and anyhow, Dinah, his wife, was going to leave him altogether if he didn't take inside work."

She had known that. Dinah had moved from Paragon Springs, had left when the depression hit in '93. Aurelia also got word now and then that her brother-in-law, Harlan, was doing well in the goldfields up north.

For a few minutes, the silence between them was thick with remembrances of old days. Then he said, "Maybe you want to see the town, rest up this evening, drive out to the claim in the morning?"

"If you don't mind, I'd like to drive out there now."

"Sure," he said, "It's only an hour or so drive. We got plenty time, plenty daylight left."

Visiting Ad's land was what she had come there for. It was nearing evening as they drove onto the Circle E ranch. The *E* was for Empire, she remembered, the name the cowboys gave their joint holdings when they took their claims. Gradually, the others sold out to Lofty but he kept the original name.

They followed a small dusty road for some time. Scissortailed fly catchers flitted in the brush along the Salt Fork River. Cattle grazed in the native grass growing between the derricks. The scatter of wooden derricks looked like big birds, she thought, pecking methodically at the ground, sucking up oil into pipes.

"This here's it," he said, stopping the automobile. He opened her door and helped her out. "Ad's claim, your land, runs from that bunch of scrub pine over here," he pointed, "to them rocks looks like sleeping elephants way off yonder there."

She stood and looked around her, then walked a few paces ahead of him. Ad's parcel looked no different from the rest of the ranch, but still, the earth beneath her feet was what he claimed, what he had died for. That old, awful time rushed back at her. As her throat started to fill, she swallowed quickly, and blinked away the tears.

The three pumping derricks were rhythmic, almost a melody in the quiet evening. Grasshoppers added their violin accompaniment.

A man came out of a little shack that squatted in the shadows cast by the first derrick. He had bark-dark skin, was dressed in shirt and dungarees. A shiver went through her when she recognized that he was Indian, probably Cherokee. She forced calm. That man had nothing to do with her past. Besides, she had heard that the Cherokee were an intelligent, civilized people.

"Jim Reese, want you to meet Miss Lucy Ann—Mrs. Walsh," Lofty introduced them. "Jim keeps an eye on things, he lives right here so's he's on hand to fix any break downs and the like."

She said quietly, "It's nice to meet you, Mr. Reese. I'm glad for the chance to thank you, in person, for your work."

He nodded, smiled, held his hat at his side. "I'm glad to meet you, Mrs. Walsh. I never met your husband, but I've heard plenty about what a good man he was. Awful shame he got killed."

"Thank you." She felt herself relaxing. "Admire would have been surprised about what's happened here. He expected to raise cattle and horses, wouldn't have guessed about the oil."

Lofty chuckled. "Sure as shootin' Ad would have been surprised! We all was, when them friends of Peter Shelby, the Pennsylvania oil man, come asking to test our land for oil. They drilled two or three dry holes. We was gettin' a pretty good laugh out of them tenderfoot engineer fellers. Then right here on Ad's land they hit the first gusher. Right here. Black clouds of oil just shootin' up and spillin' down like rain."

"It must have been a surprise and exciting."

"Oh, yeah," he answered. "One thousand barrels a day come from that one well, ever' day. It's piped down to the Shelby refinery in Enid." He said expansively, "Oklahoma oil is shipped all over the world. Now we got automobiles and steamships using petroleum and crude oil to run their engines, I don't guess the need for oil will ever run out."

"That sticky black stuff has always been good medicine for Indians," Jim Reese commented with a wry grin. "My old grandmothers used it as salve for burns, as a lubricant and as a cleanser."

"Really?" It seemed odd to her, but she understood that Indians were fairly smart in their medicines.

She looked around her, itching to be alone, thinking how she might dismiss the men but not be rude.

Reese seemed to read her mind. With a motion of his hands he asked, "Would you like to just walk around by yourself for a while, Mrs. Walsh? Or would you like one of us to show you around?"

She smiled at him. "By myself, thank you." When she moved away, the other two headed with hands in their pockets toward Reese's shack, talking.

She strolled slowly, in the twilight slanted sun, from the clump of pines to the elephant rocks. Bullbats swooped overhead, making their sounds of small thunder. The air was soft and warm. Night insects chirruped in the grass around her ankles. She climbed halfway up the first elephant back, slipped down to sit there. She sat for a while, her mind open, her body relaxed. The sky to the west was darkening. She couldn't stay long, but she wanted to feel Admire's presence, his spirit, here on his land. She waited and waited.

"Admire?" she whispered. She had hoped to gain answers from him in the same way he had given her a decent life by marrying her. She had wanted to know what he might feel she should do about the horrible scandal and Leonard's campaign. About the wealth he had given her that no one believed she could properly manage, that she wanted to put into an aeroplane factory.

After a while, a gentle breeze cooled the tears on her cheeks.

There was nothing of her husband Admire in this strange place and there never would be. He was in her heart, and she would have to take her strength from there. She was on her own.

She could hear Lofty calling her, telling her it was time they ought to head back to town. She saw his shadowy form approaching through the dark. "All right," she said, "I'm coming."

As she climbed down off the rock she told herself that she was glad she had come to Oklahoma, even if tonight hadn't turned out how she thought it might. She would ask Lofty to bring her back tomorrow and explain more how the wells worked. She wanted to visit her banker, too.

It was interesting, what Jim Reese said about how his grandmothers used crude black oil as medicine. Something about that was stirring a mess of thoughts in her mind but she couldn't sort it out to make any sense or concrete form.

Only that *in medicine and health* might be the answer to how she could help Leonard, and herself. The idea would need considerable more looking into.

"I'm ready," she told Lofty when he reached her. He took her arm, led her to where his auto loomed in wait in the moonlit dark.

Chapter Fifteen

Winslow and Osborne and likely a lot of others, too, thought that she should hide herself in shame. Believed they could use her to destroy Leonard's chances to be governor. Well, she was going to do just the opposite of what they expected. After all this time she was not about to crouch away in a dark closet. Folks were going to see more of her than they ever had, and she was going to help Leonard in his race for governor at the same time.

After her return from Oklahoma, she went to Topeka and asked for an appointment with the State Director of Public Health. Their talk turned out to be longer than scheduled, though neither of them minded. They promised to talk again soon, and as many times as necessary. From there, she went to visit two hospitals where she talked with nurses and doctors and visited patients.

Back at Paragon Springs, satisfied and well-armed, she then went to see Leonard. It was his day at the newspaper rather than in his law office.

"Lucy Ann!" he looked surprised but glad to see her as he came from the backshop into the *Echo*'s front office. He brought with him the stringent smells of paper, ink, and machines. As he closed the door behind him, the noisy *thump, slap* of the presses faded. "Nice to have you back from Oklahoma, Sis."

He waggled his inky fingers to show he couldn't touch her, then motioned for her to take the chair by the window. "Selinda is out on a story, she will be sorry to have missed you." He moved a pile of papers and sat on the corner of his desk. "What brings your dear brother the pleasure of your company? Would you like a cup of coffee? Fellows in the backshop have some on, a fresh pot."

"Thanks, no. I came to talk. Hear me out, Leonard, before you say anything." She sat up straighter, smoothed the papers in her lap. Her heart beat with excitement at her plan. "I want to campaign with you, I want to help you become governor," she told him.

His eyes widened in surprise, he started to say something, then he nodded for her to go on.

"I think we've always been of like mind about the importance of healthiness for everyone. You're trying to push laws through the legislature to prohibit fee-splitting between surgeons and family doctors and to prevent fake advertising for medical cures. Why not make better sanitation for the health of all Kansas people but especially children, one of your campaign promises? If you will, I can help."

He leaned forward, a light in his eyes. He started to touch her arm for her to continue, then withdrew his inky fingers.

"I have facts and figures, Leonard." She held up the stacks of papers in her lap. "I've talked to the head of state public health, I talked with so many doctors and nurses, I lost count. They all tell me the same thing: Children die by the hundreds, just *hundreds*, Leonard, every year. From typhoid, malaria, diarrhea, dysentery, cholera, diphtheria, worms—all caused by unclean living habits and contaminated ice, food, and water. We can change that, it doesn't have to be."

He had caught her excitement, his head bobbed eagerly. "Fine. What do you plan to do with your information? I can probably give you more. I've looked into this matter, too, hoping to do something to save lives from sickness and disease."

"I want to talk to women's groups, to anyone who will listen, about better sanitation, means to better health. Teaching facts could stop the diseases, the deaths that shouldn't happen. While I am at it, I believe I can help you, too, in your campaign."

He stood up from the desk corner, began to pace. "I agree in principle, it's a fine plan." He turned to her, his right shoulder lifted in question, "But are you sure you want to do this, Sis? You're a timid person, placing yourself in the background when around people. Are you sure you want to put yourself out there, meet the public?"

He was giving her an excuse to back out of her plan, and let it go. But she had already made up her mind. She took a deep breath and told him, "I know it will be hard for me. It will be very different from what I'm used to, but yes, I do want to go ahead. I want to show as many folks as possible the truth about me, too, Leonard. I want them to see that I'm not a dirty, deranged, mad-woman as some seem to think I must be because of what happened to me."

"If you're sure," he said, admiration glimmering in his eyes, showing in his smile. "I think it is a great plan, Sis."

She nodded and got to her feet. "The only other thing I could do, as I see it, is to hide my face, allow folks to think I am someway bad, and at the same time ignore the real good I can do. And let them defeat us. I know it's going to be hard for me to face the public, but I don't see that I have a choice. It is what I have to do."

It wouldn't hurt her confidence any, she thought, to look as nice as possible.

She could go to Topeka or even Kansas City, for a new wardrobe. She chose instead to patronize Mary Fry, a dressmaker who operated a shop in her home on a dusty side street in Paragon Springs. Mary was finely talented, could work in any large city she pleased, but she stayed in order to look after an invalid uncle, Old Seth Fry, who wouldn't leave town.

For half the morning, she and Mary pored over fashion catalogues and magazines in the small room off the parlor where Mary did her sewing. It was hard to accept some of what Mary would choose for her, linen, ribbons and lace—white, and bright colors. "I'm not a young girl, Mary. I am a mature woman. I want to look—proper, but, well, fashionable, too."

"Of course you want to look proper, and you will," Mary laughed at her. "But you're not an old crone by any means, Lucy Ann, you're still a pretty woman. You will be fashionable and sophisticated, but there's no need to look dowdy and funereal."

They compromised on three simple but stylish gowns in soft grays and blues to match her eyes and to complement her ash-blond—now mostly gray, hair. Most of the dresses were of the empire style with raised waist and shallow bodice and dolman sleeves. Lucy Ann particularly favored the tailored suits, though, that had a touch of feminine detailing and she ordered four of those. Mary would make matching cloaks and help her choose gloves, and hats to wear on the new pompadour hairstyle they decided she must have. The old coronet of braids would be changed.

Her first speech—she thought it would be good to begin at home and gain experience there—was for the Paragon Springs Ladies Aid. The group's many causes included town boosterism, aid to the poor, disaster relief, and sponsoring pleasurable social events. The women enjoyed gathering in the company of their friends for an afternoon each month, away from ordinary toil. The meeting today was being held in Aurelia's parlor. In a half circle of chairs in front of Lucy Ann, the women balanced teacups on their best-dressed knees and waited expectantly.

She sensed trouble almost from the first words out of her mouth, although among the listeners were many good friends.

The problem was, of course, that women didn't want to hear about flies and filth when they had expected to be entertained, or to be drawn into a more noble cause. Within minutes several creased brows and down-turned mouths practically begged her to be silent. She took a deep breath. They'd have to get used to it. She pushed aside nerves and continued, forthright and practical.

"Flies may seem to be harmless though annoying little creatures, but they carry disease from our stock animals to our food. Animal and human offal taints our drinking water. The main cause of infant mortality is flies and filth. And we must change that!"

People had always found flies annoying. The hungry things buzzed noisily in every room in the house. They drowned in a person's food, woke children at night so that they were cranky all next day. Sometimes smudges were fired in the evening to keep insects away so the family could sleep. But more was needed. Doors and windows must have screens to keep the flies *out*.

As she continued, she saw the women beginning to listen. To *really* hear her and start to care about her message. When she finished, they clapped heartily. Her new maroon tailored suit was soaked with perspiration under her arms and between her breasts, but she was overjoyed with the thought that she had won her first round, never mind that it had been at home with ladies she'd known for years.

★ ★ ★ ★ ★

In days to come she supplemented Leonard's speeches— he was off in another direction with his campaigning—with small, heartwarming, informative speeches of her own, promoting better health for Kansas. She spoke directly to the people in her own simple language, one of them. When she cited facts and figures, folks began to listen. And she thought, then to heed, to put into practice what they really didn't understand before.

Toilets sitting practically on top of wells, must be moved further away. Water for stock must be kept separate from that for families. Using the State Board Of Health's support, she introduced a "fly-fighters brigade" to housewives and children.

Kansas school children were to receive prizes for killing flies, being taught in the process why flies were undesirable and even dangerous. Churches were also encouraged to participate in the anti-fly campaign inaugurated by the State Board Of Health, with her help.

She argued for paper cups in schools and other institutions to replace the common drinking cup which spread so many diseases.

As she traveled around the state, lecturing, she saw a much bigger fight than she first imagined. After staying in some hotels whose sanitary practices were laggard to nil, she began to crusade for clean sheets daily on hotel beds and boiled dishes to be used in the dining room.

Her appearances were usually written up in community newspapers wherever she went. When a lecture was over, the editor or a reporter would ask her questions which she answered as fully as possible about her causes. She welcomed this as a means to spread her message in an ever-widening circle.

Often reporters tried to ask questions about her personal life, the Indian attack of her girlhood which seemed to be common knowledge all over the countryside. At that she would check her pendant watch and announce she had to be somewhere else and was running late. She didn't care to be deceptive, but she was not going to talk about herself, discuss with strangers those personal, awful times.

She persuaded people of the necessity for the Board Of Health's social surveys. Asked her audiences to please cooperate and answer the questions. For the good of all, for improvements to be made, water supply, sanitary arrangements, general cleanliness, public halls, playgrounds, recreation, housing, and business conditions, must be studied.

She wondered sometimes if she personally had always had fanatically clean habits, due to a trait handed down from her own mother, a line of German ancestors? For certain she had been strong on such since the day of the Indian attack.

Quite a few listeners in the crowds she spoke to, knew from the newspapers what had happened to her. She overheard their rumbles, "Who is she to tell us we ain't clean?" Another time, "That Indian stain gonna' always be on her, no matter how high and mighty she thinks she is." And again, "Puttin' on airs like some churchy saint!"

As much as such comments made her cringe, made her want to hide away, she persisted on the path she had set for herself.

Word spread of the good she was attempting to do and she was welcomed more often, by a variety of groups but mostly women's organizations. People wanted to know the ways and means they could help themselves to better health. From whomever could give them clear facts. Far too many Kansas families had lost a child, in some cases several of their children, to typhoid, diphtheria, malaria. They hadn't dreamed that those horrible diseases might have been prevented. Could be stopped from ever happening again.

It was a rare woman who hadn't lost a child in its infancy. Or a husband his wife, in childbirth. If conditions at the birthing, and after, had been more sanitary, chances were that many of those babies, many of those wives would have lived.

She explained how, if no other methods were available, they must sterilize needles and instruments over a hot flame at the stove, gauze and cloths in a hot oven. Water needed to be boiled, and there should be no scrimping on the use of soap and water in a sickroom, or simply in the home to prevent sickness, ever. She preached soap and water until she thought she'd have no voice left.

Child-bed fever, or puerperal fever, a very dangerous disease that killed new mothers, could be eliminated altogether if sanitary, aseptic, procedures were followed.

As often as she was listened to at her speeches and applauded for her efforts, she was equally often ostracized and called names. Sometimes she was the target of thrown garbage. More than once she mopped rotted cabbage and tomatoes off her face and clothes and persisted in talking. In those instances there was always someone in the crowd, some right-thinking good individual, who would persuade the tormentor to stop.

She discovered that she could pass on her information in normal conversation at parties and other social affairs—when she could convince folks to listen to the subject of filth and flies. When a listener was won over, she felt re-

warded. Those who disliked what she had to say, might still
think it over at home and later come around, she told herself. She wouldn't give up.

Whenever there was an opportunity, she slipped in a few
words about her brother's good qualities and what he meant
to do for the state if named governor in next year's election.
She began to enjoy what she was doing. If she could truly
make a difference, she would ever be glad she had taken on
the battle. Even if Leonard didn't win, although she hoped
he would.

On her infrequent and brief visits home, she found
things ably managed by Lucas. She raised his pay, and hired
him full time. Her family was a little surprised that she had
turned into a "speechifying woman" but supported her efforts and helped Davis out on her farm when he needed an
extra hand.

Time and again Tom left notes at her place. She answered in brief notes of her own: as soon as she could she
wanted to see him and learn "the way of the wind" with his
aeroplanes. But for now she owed her time to Leonard and
to the fight she was in.

She spoke at a barbecue in Beloit, Kansas, that drew
some twelve thousand people. Of course they were there
mainly for the food and managed to consume three thousand pounds of meat, twenty-five-hundred loaves of bread,
and fifteen-hundred gallons of coffee!

She spoke at a watermelon carnival in Abilene. Many of
the folks, swatting flies and eating their way through twenty
tons of watermelons, stopped to hear her speak from her
soapbox. And God willing, took home new information that
could help them. It had been fairly simple to point out the
fly problem.

While in Abilene, she considered investing in real estate there. It was pretty country on the western edge of the Flint Hills. The incredible crop of watermelons, she learned, had increased the value of the sandhills from five dollars to *fifty dollars* an acre!

After a few very busy weeks she recognized that she needed a rest. At least a short time back on the farm to soothe her soul, restore her vitality before continuing her lectures. So she was glad her last speech for a while would be at Paragon Springs on Labor Day.

The celebration began as always with a parade through the dusty streets, followed by an all-day show of trades and crafts, a string of political speeches from various parties. Leonard was away speaking in Wichita with a hope to gain votes from there. She would represent him on their home ground. Her first lecture at home had been to that small group of ladies in Aurelia's parlor, this was a chance to speak to a much larger crowd.

When it was her turn at the lecture platform, she stepped up and was introduced to the crowd by Meg, who, in spite of a few crow's feet around her eyes, was slender as a girl in her navy suit. Lucy Ann returned Meg's encouraging smile, began her speech as always, detailing the dangers of the lack of sanitation, how diseases came about. She had scarcely gotten started when a male voice shouted from the crowd, "Ain't you got no shame, Lucy Ann Walsh? Go on home, woman, where you never shoulda left."

It was grizzled Mr. Potter, who always looked at the negative, was against whatever proposition was afoot. He was standing next to E. C. "Easy" Osborne.

Osborne shook his head, "I don't think folks want to

hear no toilet talk, Mrs. Walsh. Better take Potter's suggestion and go on home."

Aurelia, her tall flower and feather-stacked bonnet waving in the wind, pushed her way through the crowd to stand next to the men. You could hear her sizzling anger over most of the fairgrounds, "You hush, Potter, and you, Easy, before I stuff my gloves down your throats!"

Lucy Ann began again.

Easy Osborne shouted, "Some of you might not know that woman up there. That's Lucy Ann Walsh, the woman the Injuns did it to."

His words struck more severe than any garbage ever thrown. Her knees weakened and she was afraid she couldn't stand. She wanted to flee but her body had frozen. Through a kind of sick haze she saw Owen and Hamilton move up beside Aurelia. At her order, "Remove Potter and Easy from the grounds for public disturbance! If they give you trouble, let them cool their heels in the jail." She had the authority, she was mayor, had been for years.

An argument seemed to be taking place, with Osborne and Potter finally agreeing to keep their mouths shut.

Even so, the damage was done. Half of the audience was drifting away in small groups, grumbling and whispering in shock as they went, looking back over their shoulders at her. Easy and Potter stalked off ahead of them, their job completed.

Lucy Ann, sickened, was about to leave the stage when Meg hissed in her ear, "Don't you quit now, Lucy Ann! Don't you let them win."

"What—?" She stood, trembling, and stared out at the remnants of her audience. "There's so few to listen—"

"You just keep talking, and don't you stop 'til you're finished on your own."

So, somehow, she kept talking. She stood her spot and said her piece. When she finished, the listeners that were left, mostly her friends, applauded loudly. She thought it was for staying as much as for what she'd had to say.

"I'm sorry that happened, Lucy Ann," Aurelia said to her later as she stepped down from the stage. "Sometimes I think that blessed man Potter ought to be hanged, and Easy with him."

"Oh, I—" her response was stopped by Meg giving her a hard hug. "You did it! I'm so glad you didn't give in to those sanctimonious scalawags."

"I'm sorry so many folks left," Emmaline approached to say. "You've got some important things to say, Lucy Ann, and you're better at it every day. I was worried for a minute Potter and Easy might stir folks up to hurt you physically."

She shook her head, realized how very tired she was, how glad she was to be among friends. She said wryly, "At least they didn't pelt me with spoiled cabbages as has happened. I won't say I'm getting used to it, exactly, but something like today happens pretty much everywhere I go."

Chapter Sixteen

Lucy Ann was in her rain-soaked field, picking kafir under gray skies. Taffy was hitched to her wagon beyond the row. She looked up to see a buggy halted beside her house and a man in a dark suit crossing the fields toward her. She hoped he wasn't a traveling salesman. She didn't need anything, except to be out there, working. A cool breeze blew as she waited. There was the rustle of field mice off to her left.

"Mrs. Walsh?"

"Yes, I'm Lucy Ann Walsh."

"I am Lester Elroy, from the *Kansas City Daily News*."

Good Heavens! He'd come a far piece if it was just to talk to her. He was a nice looking young man. She liked newspapermen, her brother was one, among other occupations. She liked that she could champion her causes in the newspapers.

"How can I help you?" She wiped her wet palms several times on her apron, shook his hand.

"I'm here for a story, Mrs. Walsh, if you'll consent. I think it is important for readers to know your personal story. The truth of your life—"

She felt a chill, then a flash of anger. She frowned. "Did Philander Winslow send you here by any chance?" He was losing in the race, he might still be trying to ruin Leonard through her. She snatched an ear of kafir corn off the stalk.

"Good Lord, no! That pompous, greedy, rumor-monger? No, just the opposite. I'm here because I think your story needs to be told. Not just about your causes, good health and so on, but about *you*."

166

"No, I don't think so, Mr. Elroy, I'd rather not talk about my personal life. It's regretful you've come all this way for nothing." She tossed the stubby ear of kafir into her wagon.

"You're a very interesting person, Mrs. Walsh." He trailed along behind her as she continued stripping ears of kafir from the stalk and tossing them past him into her wagon. "A Kansas pioneer." He ducked as an ear of kafir flew by him. "A woman who survived an Indian attack when several other family members were killed. Sister to one of Kansas's finest candidates for public office. You give freely of your time to help end one of society's major health problems, lack of sanitation—"

She hesitated, thought it over. "Would you like to come into the house, Mr. Elroy?" She liked some of what he was saying, about Leonard, about her causes. She liked his sincere honest looks. Maybe she could skirt around any talk about herself, keep details about her personal life brief and still give him a story that would help Leonard and Kansas in general.

She led him to the house and into her parlor, brought him a cup of coffee. Then she vanished for a few moments to perform a quick wash up, change her dress, comb her hair and whip it into a pompadour. When she returned, he was looking around the room and making notes.

"It's just a woman's parlor, Mr. Elroy. Like anyone's," she said politely.

"Yes," he said with a smile, "that's exactly what I was writing down."

Good start, she thought. *He was going to write that she was quite civilized, for all that had happened to her.*

"What is it you would like to know, Mr. Elroy?" She sat down across from him, and laced her corn-roughened fingers in her lap.

"I've read many accounts of atrocities against settlers at the hands of Indians in Western Kansas in the 1860's and 1870's. Men, women, and children murdered. Scores of women brutally assaulted. I remember particularly the accounts written about the capture of two young women, Sarah White and Anna Brewster Morgan by Sioux warriors in Western Kansas in the early seventies."

She nodded guardedly. "I've heard about them—and about other women who suffered the same as —" *Me*. Indian raids were too common then. Men were scalped and murdered, women and horses were usually taken captive. There wasn't a woman on the frontier who didn't live in daily fear of being taken.

Miss White, eighteen, and Mrs. Morgan, a new bride, were captured by Indians a month apart in the fall. At the time both of their families were murdered. They found themselves in the same Indian camp and, on one occasion, managed to escape almost to Dodge before they were found and taken back. For months, they suffered extreme cruelty and hard usage from the Indians, although Mrs. Morgan married an Indian chief as the lesser of two evils, believing the other to be her death.

General George Armstrong Custer and his troops traced them and traded for their release by promising to free five captured Indian chiefs that were going to be hanged. Mrs. Morgan, it was said, was sorry to be found and had a hard time fitting back into her old life. Her mind gradually failed and she died in an asylum. Miss White, on the other hand, considered her months in captivity an ordeal well over, told her story to newspapers, later married a good man, and let time help her to forget as best she could.

Was that the sort of thing he wanted to know and write up about her in his newspaper? *Lord help her*. It was her own fault. By campaigning in public these past months she had perched herself for the arrow of trouble like a wild turkey out on a bare limb. Sooner or later it was bound to happen, somebody wanting to delve deeper into the worst nightmare of her life. Bring it *all* back, not just the surface ugly stories that were circulating.

He was saying, "Would you share the events of that day your family was attacked? Tell us about the outrage?"

She trembled, squeezed her hands tighter together. "To what good, Mr. Elroy? You see, I've spent most of my life trying to overcome what happened. To put it out of my mind." An inner stubbornness mushroomed. Not for the world would she breathe a word that would harm Rachel, or hurt Leonard's chances to be governor. If she said anything at all, how could she avoid that?

"I understand, Mrs. Walsh. My reason for asking for your story from you directly, is that there have been so many different accounts of what happened to you. Lurid stories, but each so different from the other they hardly make sense. I feel the real story should come from you. For instance, one account claimed that after you were captured you wanted to marry your attacker and continue to live with his tribe as an Indian. Is that true?"

She shook her head. "That is holy nonsense. Rubbish! I was never captured, for one thing. I never lived a day with the Indians. Help for my brother Leonard and I came in time, thank heaven, though not for the rest of my family who were killed. And the raid took place in Nebraska, before we came to Kansas." She sighed. Unfortunately, the stories were already out there. She might as well, as he said, set them straight. It was hard to see, though, how it would do any good.

"It was as pretty a day as a body could expect in early

spring in Nebraska," she told Elroy. "Papa was out plowing, I was carrying water back from the creek, my older brother was further up the creek cutting wood. The warriors, or renegades as they were, came to the house. They behaved friendly at first. Mama fed them. Then they took a liking to a rose-pattern china pitcher that had belonged to my grandmother in Bavaria. Mama—Mama—"

How could she explain the terror of that day so he could understand it? Her own heart was practically standing still in its beat, remembering. The old horror had returned like a hundred-mile wind.

When she was able to, she went on huskily, "The rose pitcher was all Mama had left of that time. She wanted—to keep it. They—the savages hacked her to pieces when she fought them. My brother, Leonard, we called him Laddie back then when he was just a little boy, saw it from where he hid up on a rafter. The Indians ransacked the house, destroyed everything they didn't want, tracked Mama's blood everywhere.

"Out in the field, Papa heard our screams. He came, fired on the Indians and killed one of them. The rest circled on him, and beat and butchered him to death. They killed my older brother the same when he came to help. They bashed the heads of my baby sisters against the side of the cabin, killing them. One warrior grabbed me, the other grabbed Laddie when they heard him sob up on the rafter."

She drew a long shuddering breath, wasn't sure she could tell the rest. "I won't speak of the hostiles' attack on me except to say that I was beaten severely and I—I was outraged. I saw that they were starting to scalp Laddie, alive, when everything turned dark to me. When I returned to consciousness, neighbors had arrived. They had shot and killed the savages.

"If help hadn't come when it did, I'm sure Leonard and I would be dead, or worse, would have been taken captive."

Elroy looked at her for a long time. There was a shine of tears in his youthful eyes. He hadn't said a word while she talked and now it looked like he wouldn't be able to talk for a minute or two yet.

Finally, he said in a low voice, "But you survived and managed a normal life. Both of you, Mrs. Walsh, you and Leonard. You didn't let what happened destroy you, nor should others destroy you for it. You went on, not just for yourselves but to help others, to help your state. That's how I'm going to write your story, that will be my theme. I feel honored to be the one to write this, Mrs. Walsh."

"Well, thank you for that," she answered him after a moment. She was glad the telling was over. She considered, after a sip of coffee, "Mr. Elroy, would you like to hear more of our story? I have a friend I would like for you to talk to. Her name is Mrs. Meg Gibbs. She can tell you the facts about the shooting Leonard was involved in when he was a boy. The facts are not as some, Philander Winslow, for one, are claiming."

"Today?" He looked as though she were handing him a key to a golden kingdom.

"I don't know about today. It depends on if Meg is busy. I will tell you how to find her. I'm sure she will be glad to talk to you. Just tell her that I sent you."

He touched his pencil to his tongue and began to write on his pad of paper. She refilled his coffee cup, brought him a slice of apple pie.

It was hard, but with effort she pulled her mind from the dark halls of memory where she had never wanted to be again. She sat quietly, her own pie untouched. He scribbled away, filling page after page, stopping now and then to eat a

171

forkful of pie and take a drink of coffee.

Finally, she said, "Before you go, if you don't mind, let's talk a bit about aviation, possibly for another of your newspaper stories." It felt as good as a warm soothing bath, a flood of sunshine, to return to affairs of the present and she released a long sigh. "I believe the aeroplane is going to be very good for our country, don't you? Being able to fly will make wonderful changes that will benefit us all in ways we can only now imagine. How do you feel about that, Mr. Elroy?"

Mr. Elroy's story was printed on the second page of the *Kansas City Daily News* the following week. He sent Lucy Ann a copy. The story was as different from earlier accounts about her and Leonard as day was from night.

Mr. Elroy had realized something important that the other writers had missed. It was true readers liked lurid tales of violence, but they liked even more stories of heroism, courage, honor and especially, *hope*. He had turned their story around.

It was amazing, she thought, that facts about folks could be told so differently.

After Elroy's story appeared, other stories about her and Leonard began to be told in a different, more favorable, light. One day they were villified in print as criminals, practically, the next they were heroes, pillars of the community, patterns for decency.

Whether the change would have any lasting concrete good, remained to be seen. But she felt better. As much as she disliked having her private story told, it was a cleansing, too. She wrote Elroy a note of gratitude. And went back to her speaking tours.

She was on the road most of the winter. She felt that

now she had begun, she mustn't let up until everyone in the state had gotten and understood her message.

The catcalls and throwing of objects at her gradually ceased, leaving only the winter weather to give her difficulty. She took whatever transportation she could, traveling by sleigh, train, and sometimes a host's automobile when roads were clear enough.

In April, Paragon Springs's and then Topeka's merchants by the score adopted her plan and were paying children one cent for every two flies killed. It was a necessary effort to kill the flies in early spring before others could hatch out. Merchants in other towns quickly followed suit.

Her younger grandchildren invited her to their school to discuss her slate of health programs. Their classmates were excited at earning pennies for killing nuisance flies. Marcus and Amy took the opportunity to show her their special projects. Along with other children across the state, they were testing seed corn by the "rag-baby" or blotter method. Grains of corn were placed between wet cloths and blotters and kept in a warm place to sprout.

She loved Zachary, Marcus, and Amy with her very soul. She wanted so much for them to have a grand future in the place where they were born. She still believed an aeroplane factory was the answer to the town's future. But she had not seen Tom in months, except at a distance, one or the other of them taking off for somewhere at a constant rate.

Then they chanced to meet one spring day in Wurst's general market in town. A current of unspoken thoughts and feelings filled the space between them.

"Thank goodness we both have to eat," Tom exclaimed, "we'd never see one another, otherwise."

She laughed, although her heart was pounding and she couldn't seem to swallow. She had missed him, missed knowing about his flying. He had probably made all kinds of progress with aeroplane building and she hadn't yet told him she wanted a factory. "I've been busy—" she said lamely.

"I know." He grinned. "If I couldn't see you, at least I was able to read about you in the papers." There was much affection in his expression, his voice was throaty with emotion, "You're a fine woman, Lucy Ann, to live through all you have and be so strong. Strong enough to help others the way you are, and let the chips fall."

Despite his praise, a knot of anxiety formed in her stomach. She wished he hadn't learned *everything* about her. If her and Leonard's past hadn't become a tool in political battle, to be picked up by newspapers, he might never have known about the Indian episode of her life. She would never have told him. She liked their bond the way it was, just close friends, and no need to share dark secrets.

She swallowed a dryness in her throat. "How have you been, Tom? You must be keeping busy, too. Joey tells me you are flying all over the place these days, to one meet after another all last summer and fall and this past winter, too. He said folks are turning out in droves to see the *Paragon Spirit I* and *Spirit II*, and that they are quite taken and excited by them."

"As they should be," he said, with a show of pride. His blue eyes glittered. "I've spent most of the winter building the *New Spirit II* and you have to see it! It's another double-seater, a beauty that flies like a dream."

"It sounds grand, Tom." She began to relax, felt like her old self with him again.

"It is grand," he said, again with honest pride. "I'm going to take it to the skies around the middle of May at an airshow in Larned. I want you to promise me you won't be gone off somewhere. I'm going to be there a couple of days ahead of time so I want you to meet me there. You're going for your first aeroplane ride. This time I won't take no for an answer."

Although her heart lunged at his declaration, she summoned a quiet, noncommittal smile. "We'll see." She had plenty of time to think of an excuse *not* to fly, if she wasn't "off somewhere" and once more couldn't manage the nerve to go up with him.

Chapter Seventeen

The Larned meet was held as always in a large open field. Horse-drawn rigs and autos lined the far edges of the field. A good-sized crowd had gathered, likely from all over the western part of the state.

There were at least a half dozen aeroplanes and their pilots that would be performing.

Lucy Ann found Tom. As he had said, his *New Spirit* was a beauty. Looking the craft over, Lucy Ann decided that she had lived a fair good life if it should end this day, but her pleasure would never be complete until she flew. Besides, the aeroplane looked substantial, or anyway more safe than any Tom had built before.

When their turn came, though, her heart climbed into her throat. Her knees turned to jelly as Tom helped her into the rear seat and buckled her in.

"Hey, look!" a farmer just beyond the rope barrier shouted, "that woman is going up in the aeroplane, too!" Others came running to see.

She settled herself, tied over her pompadour and hat the scarf Tom handed back to her. She did her best to calm her nerves, tried not to think that this might be her last day on earth.

He smiled over his shoulder at her, gave a thumbs up, and started the engine.

She had never felt such terror as the craft roared, rumbled, and trembled around her. *Dear God, what did I let myself in for?* She hung on for dear life.

Behind the rope barrier off to the side, the gathering

crowd had grown. "Woman's going up!" they were shouting, clapping. "Hey, a woman's going up!"

Foolish woman, she thought, *foolish, foolish woman.*

Then they were jerking, lurching, then traveling along the ground more smoothly, at unbelievable speed. Surely as fast as a horse, or an automobile, maybe as fast as lightning. Her heart stopped. Then they were off the ground and in the air, climbing. In the air, the aeroplane felt very small, no bigger than a large man's coffin. And it could be hers.

They went up, up. And gradually she began to feel a thrill of excitement. Her hand went to her chest and she smiled. Tom was motioning for her to look down. But she couldn't. Could she? She looked down, and gasped. The people below looked as small as infants. They were waving their arms, cheering. Far around them were fields that looked like bed quilts. She lifted her arm in a quick little wave to the crowd below and then yanked it back to hang on, again.

They circled around and around in the blue sky, the pure sweet air. Then, from the position of the sun, they headed in a slight southwest direction. The plane engine purred, the wind was cool. She had made Tom promise to do no fancy tricks.

After a while, he motioned again for her to look down. She did. And she saw her town, Paragon Springs, below them. She looked again, to be sure. In her wildest dreams she would never have thought she would see it this way. There it was, a play town, with little streets, houses and stores. There was the Drug Store and Hospital, Wurst's Grocery and the Community Bank. Sweet heaven, there was Aurelia's house, and the toy person hanging clothes in the backyard was Aurelia!

She wanted to shout down to her, tell her to look up and

177

see Lucy Ann riding in an aeroplane. Time enough, and she would tell her!

She wanted to find Meg's house, Leonard and Selinda's, her children's. Tom must have guessed, or wanted all along to show her. One by one, they flew over houses and farms she recognized—strange that she could recognize them, she thought—from the air and so high up.

Later, she could hardly remember the ride back to Larned or landing. She had kept her eyes closed most of the time, descending. For the most part they had sailed down smoothly. She had hardly felt the bump, bump, bump as they came to a chugging stop.

Tom shut off the engine and climbed down from the plane. He helped her out. She was glad to have solid ground under her jellied legs and feet again at the same time her heart pumped with excitement. Folks seemed to be cheering as much for her, brave enough to go up in the aeroplane, as for Tom and his magical craft.

She straightened her shoulders and took a deep breath. She looked at Tom. "I have never, ever, had so grand a time in my life! Thank you. It was wonderful, so exciting, I just don't know how to tell you how much I liked it. And I was scared, Tom, I was really scared in the beginning."

"You are welcome," he said, and with a very strange soft look in his eyes, he kissed her mouth. "Thank you for flying with me."

There was something heady in the silence that followed, and then suddenly, while she was still trying to decipher what had just happened, and what she ought to do next, a reporter rushed up with a pad and pencil. He asked Tom rapid-fire questions about the Paragon *New Spirit*, then asked him to introduce his wife.

Her face warmed, and she frowned. Tom had the audacity to grin at her but he remained unruffled. He said, "Mrs. Walsh is a good friend, not my wife. We share an interest in aeroplanes. Surely, you've heard of Lucy Ann Walsh? She is campaigning for better health in Kansas, and her brother, Representative Leonard Voss, from Hodgeman County, is running for governor."

Her heart sank. She worried what the reporter might write about her and Tom. She didn't want gossip to start up again. *That silly kiss.*

He began to ask her questions. She answered honestly, briefly, about her interest in aviation, how Tom was a neighbor and that started her interest. She talked about Leonard and his programs, plus her own causes.

She privately prayed she wasn't hurting Leonard's chances, simply because she wanted a ride in her good friend's aeroplane.

"So your brother, Leonard Voss, plans to be the Progressive Party nominee for governor? I've heard that Henry J. Allen, from Wichita is aiming for the same, as well as a fellow named Winslow. Does he think he can beat them?"

She was sure he could win over Winslow. Philander's silken finery and underhanded ways contrasted unfavorably with the down-to-earth honest simplicity of her brother and Allen. Whether Leonard could beat Henry Allen she wasn't quite as sure. "Leonard will leave that to the voters to decide," she said diplomatically. She would have preferred to praise her brother, but she was still too shaky from the aeroplane ride to engage in a political debate.

Despite her enjoyment of the plane ride, she decided it best to stay clear of Tom's company for a while. There was something going on between them she wasn't quite sure about. Plus, she didn't want to be responsible for the start-up of unsavory talk again. With the help of newspaper articles before her aeroplane ride, public sentiment was starting to lean in Leonard's favor.

It wasn't fair to Tom, so proud of his work and wanting to show it to her, but it had to be. His kiss that day had been innocent, at least she finally chose to think it was, but heaven only knew what the public might make of something like that, and at her age. She wanted no more scandals in her name.

There were too many people already, her family among them, who found it hard to believe that she and Tom were only friends. No use to give them fodder for their mills.

A month later she was there when the Progressive Party met in Emporia and put up a full state ticket.

She sat back and listened to Leonard's impassioned speech. He never failed to inspire her and make her proud. At the end of his talk he quoted "A Kansas Creed" recently written by Kansas author, Charles Harger:

"We believe in Kansas, in the glory of her prairies, in the richness of her soil, in the beauty of her skies and in the healthfulness of her climate.

"We believe in the Kansas people, in their sturdy faith and abounding enthusiasm, in their patriotism and the good things in civilization, in their respect for law and their love of justice, in their courage and zeal, in their independence and in their devotion to uplifting influences in education and religion.

"We believe in Kansas institutions, in the Kansas language and in Kansas ideals, in her cleanliness of society and in her demand that honor, sobriety, and respect be maintained in public and in private life, in her marvelous productiveness and in her wondrous future.

"We pledge that by thought and deed we will magnify

our state and her people, spread the word of her greatness to all the world, maintain in our homes and in our communities a standard of living that shall be honored by all, develop our schools and churches to a yet higher plane, open hospitable arms to all people who seek to build homes and industries, aid nature that the bounty of the soil will yield greater fruit, connect our communities by highways that will invite a large acquaintance with the state's splendid possibilities and make our commonwealth a haven of prosperity and happiness.

"We pledge that as citizens we will look on the bright side of existence and ever strive to shed cheer, that we will be loyal to Kansas folks and to Kansas's institutions, that we will try to correct evils rather than complain of wrong conditions and will lend a hand to those who are endeavoring to banish sorrow and want and crime from this earth.

"We pledge that as the pioneers made Kansas the child of freedom, we, their sons and daughters, will maintain the spirit of their teachings, see for her people a life of full reward, give a service that shall bring happiness into every home and make this commonwealth the fairest in the galaxy of states!"

She was sure Leonard would win. And what better contribution could Paragon Springs as a town make to Kansas's present and future, than her brother in the governor's chair?

Simply because he was from Paragon Springs, and her, too, their town was getting mention in newspapers far and wide. Fortunately it was now favorable mention.

The time was right, she thought, to launch the aeroplane factory and put their town solidly on the map. It was time to light a lamp on the wonderful town that turned out Leonard.

Galvanized, the very next day she invited Tom to supper. After they'd eaten, she told him she wanted to provide the money for the new commerce, an aeroplane manufacturing plant that would employ a great many people to build and sell his aeroplanes. Her one stipulation to the use of her money was that the factory must be built at Paragon Springs.

After his initial surprise that she wanted to be involved, he declared with feeling, "I've wanted to do this for a long time, myself. And why not now, why not here? I wouldn't have any objection." He grinned. "My farm isn't productive although you've tried to help. It only makes sense to build an aeroplane factory on the land."

They sat at her table until the oil in the lamp burned low, discussing and drawing plans for the factory. They listed equipment they would need, the number of planes that could be turned out in a year and the probable cost, and how many workers would be needed for the assembly. "We'll need others' expertise on this," Tom said, "right from the beginning."

The name of the company, of course, would be *Paragon Springs Aviation*. "We'll need to operate a flying school, too," he said. "There's no use to produce aeroplanes if no one knows how to fly them." His entire farm would be one large flying field.

Dawn was silvering the sky outside her kitchen window when they finally shook hands, satisfied. He continued to hold her hand. His palm was warm around hers, and it felt nice, dangerously nice.

She laughed, embarrassed. "Goodness, but we've lost track of time! It'll be time to do the milking in another hour."

"Lucy Ann, dear, I've enjoyed making these plans with

you." He looked tired but exultant, there were shadows under his eyes, the stubble of whiskers on his jaw. He pulled her hand up to hold it against his chest. She could feel the thumping beat of his heart and it strangely seemed to match her own. He said, "I always enjoy being with you, we have such good times together." His glance was warm, hungry. "This past year when you were so busy, I felt like a lost pup, I missed you so."

All at once she was frightened to death of what he might say next. She said hurriedly, avoiding his eyes, "I've missed our times together, too, Tom, but I had a lot to do." She tried to pull her hand away but he lifted it to his whiskery cheek and then kissed her palm. She felt rattled, shaken. "Tom, please, don't—"

"Wait, Lucy Ann, listen to me." His voice was husky. He cupped her shoulders in his broad hands. "I've never cared for another person the way I care for you. I am in love with you. I know I should court you proper before I ask but I don't want to wait. Tonight was very special. Please, dear Lucy Ann, marry me? I would be so honored to have you for my wife."

She stood a moment in embarrassment, in shock, and yet a little pleased. It was flattering to have him want to marry her, and her so much older—and he so handsome and a man any woman would love to have for a husband. A time or two in the last year or so she had guessed this moment might come, then she had dismissed the thought as foolishness. It was difficult, now, to be sensible.

"I'm fond of you, too, Tom. You've been a good friend. But you are so much younger than me." A new thought came to her. "If it's money for the factory you're thinking of, you don't have to marry me for that. I'm glad to provide the money. Although it will be an investment on which I expect a high return, for myself, for the town, and for you."

His dark eyebrows knitted, a shine of anger touched his eyes. He released her. "Is that what you think? That I believe I should marry you for money for the plant?" He stood back, clearly hurt. He shoved his hands in his pockets. "That's hogwash, Lucy Ann. How can you think it? I love you, deeply, that's why I want you to marry me. Damn it, I have money of my own. My grandparents were very generous in their wills. The difference in our ages doesn't matter. We get along very well, we have fun together, you know we do. We are a match. We could make a fine marriage and build our factory at the same time." The expression on his face again looked hopeful.

Her feelings hedged a bit, and for a fleeting second she wanted to give in. She fought the feeling. He might be right that they could succeed in marriage as well as in a business partnership. Maybe, if marriage was what both wanted.

She looked at him, and fought a stinging in her eyes. The truth was, she didn't want to get married again. Admire was a good man, and she had no regrets that she had spent every hour of every day trying to please him, grateful to him for marrying her. But she was only now learning who she really was, and what she wanted. She liked her independence, doing what she pleased, her own way. That independence was one treasure she wasn't ready to risk losing.

"I'm touched that you asked me to marry you, Tom. And I guess I wasn't really thinking when I—spoke about the money. I—don't hardly know what to say now. You are one of the finest, most interesting men I'll ever know. I care for you, truly. But I still have to say *no* to marriage."

He nodded, but he looked as though she had destroyed him. He turned his back, seemed to gather his feelings together.

She spoke to his back, his broad shoulders, fought an urge to touch him. She spoke through a tight, aching throat, "I want the factory very much, Tom, and I want to be part of the company. I hope this won't change our business agreement."

"Sure." He shrugged and slowly turned around. His smile was as engaging as ever, if a little thin around the edges. "I won't say I'm not disappointed that you turned me down. We love one another, and we could make a great married couple, I still believe. But if it is business only, it is business only." He caught her hands, held them tightly a moment, seemed to be fighting something deep inside him. Then he kissed her cheek in brotherly fashion, and was gone.

As the door closed behind him, a chasm bloomed painfully in her heart. She experienced an overwhelming feeling of loneliness, of loss beyond measure. She couldn't breathe, couldn't think. She started for the door to call him back, then she looked for a chair to sit down.

She sat with her head in her hands, her fingers getting wet from her tears of frustration and confusion. She hadn't been prepared for this, not this. As wonderful, funny, and enjoyable as Tom was to be with, she couldn't have truly fallen in love with him, could she? In the name of Sweet Reason, she was a middle-aged woman. She'd had one good man in her life, and that ought to be enough.

She carefully shut away the singing in her heart, knowing how reckless it would be to look at what the answer might be to her question.

She looked at the door and calm resolve settled over her. She would be practical. There was the aeroplane factory and the town to think about, first and foremost. They would both get over this other—this unfortunate attraction for one another, they must.

Chapter Eighteen

Her new telephone was a strange contraption, although Lucy Ann thought she ought to have one now that she was a business-woman. She cranked the handle for central, listened, then asked to be connected to the Symington residence in town. Three long rings and two shorts sounded over the line. Aurelia had had a telephone for almost two years.

"Hello?" Aurelia's voice sounded as if she were at the bottom of a barrel.

"Aurelia," she shouted back, "I want you to go for a ride with me over to Flagg. Can you go?"

"Flagg? There's hardly anything there anymore. Why would you want to go to Flagg?"

"I know there's not much there, that's why I want to go. I'll explain when I stop for you. You're going? I need to talk to you about something else, and we can talk on the way."

After she picked up Aurelia in her buggy, Lucy Ann got them on the road again, urging Taffy on with a click of her tongue. "I'm going to buy an automobile one of these days," she told Aurelia. "A Model T Ford like yours."

Aurelia turned to stare at her. "You, Lucy Ann? A motorcar?"

"Yes. This horse and buggy business is too slow. If you're going to travel on the ground it might as well be by auto. Much faster."

"I declare. Well, Owen and I do enjoy our motorcar—"

"It's going to be even better to travel by air in an aeroplane, of course. The world is changing very fast, Aurelia," she said, looking over at her. "We might as well try to keep up." They hit a bump in the road and both of them bounced a little on the slick leather seat. A brown thrasher flew up from a clump of roadside weeds. Taffy shied, then continued in a steady lope.

"Does what you're talking about have something to do with why we're going to Flagg?" Aurelia wanted to know. She tucked a silvery, wind-loosened tendril of hair back in place under her hat.

"Yes, it does." She gave the driving reins a snap and Taffy's hooves clip-clopped on the dirt road. "I thought you in particular would like to be along when I buy up what's left of that old abandoned town. There was a time those folks over there gave you a blessed hard time, when they fought us here at Paragon Springs over which town was going to be county seat."

"You're going to buy two or three old empty buildings? What in heaven's name for?"

"Just some handy extra buildings for the Paragon Springs Aviation Company. The main hangar will be new, of course, and built of brick—"

"Whoa! New hangar? Aviation Company? What on earth are you talking about, Lucy Ann Walsh? What have you and that man done?"

"Tom Reilly, if that is who you mean by *that man,* and I, are forming a partnership in Paragon Springs's first aviation company. It's fairly simple, really, but Aurelia, there's more I have to tell you."

"You're getting married? To that man!"

She took a breath to steady herself, "No, I'm not marrying Tom, but if I wanted, I could. He asked." She hurried on to Aurelia's stunned look. "We're business partners, that's all, so don't fret. This factory is going to mean a lot to Paragon Springs, Aurelia. That's why I wanted you to be the first to know. This is your town, almost more than anyone's. You have worked hard toward Paragon Springs's survival. And I've wanted for quite a while to do my part. This is it. Aviation, I've decided, is the answer. Bless the Lord that there is the oil money from Ad's land to pay for it until the company is earning on its own."

"Oil money—from Ad's land?" Aurelia looked close to apoplexy. She rasped, like she could use a drink of water, "Lucy Ann, you never said—!"

"I'm sorry I haven't told you about this before, Aurelia. You probably deserved to know, you're one of my dearest friends. Maybe keeping the money a secret to myself hasn't been one of the smartest things I've done, but that's how I wanted to do it. I just wanted the time to be right, I wanted to reach some decisions on my own, and well, that's how it is."

"For heaven's sake, Lucy Ann, I don't know what to think! Tell me everything. Does Meg know?" She looked suspicious, jealous.

"Only my family has heard of it, 'til now. First there was the lease money, and then oil was discovered on Ad's claim . . ."

The Flagg buildings were brought to Tom's farm and set where the main headquarters of Paragon Springs Aviation would be. With fresh paint and repairs, they would be used as offices or tool sheds.

Lumber, brick, and other building materials arrived by railroad car from the east within a couple of weeks, and were then freighted by several wagons out to the new company site.

A fleet of bricklayers, carpenters and other tradesmen, most of them hired from the Paragon Springs area and surrounding communities, arrived to build the hangars and prepare the landing fields.

Construction commenced immediately. With so many at work, the factory and hangars being built changed the look of Tom's farm practically overnight.

Tom brought a friend, another flyer, Billy Calvert, for Lucy Ann to meet. "I'd like to make Billy a chief engineer, if you agree, Lucy Ann. Billy graduated in civil engineering from the University of Kansas at Lawrence. Since then he has also had some experience managing a machine and foundry company."

"It's nice to meet you, Mr. Calvert." She shook his hand, giving him the once over at the same time.

He had removed his tweed cap, and he bowed slightly over their hands. "Mrs. Walsh." He had wavy dark auburn hair, snapping blue eyes, and wore an almost constant wide grin. He was a lot younger than either of them, maybe in his late twenties.

"It's nice to know of your experience and learning, Mr. Calvert. I suppose like most young men nowadays you've been interested in flying since you saw your first dirigible?"

"You bet. I've been interested in engines, too, since I was a tad. Built my first engine when I was fifteen. Made a mistake testing it indoors, though. It sucked the wallpaper plumb off the walls and ceiling of my mother's house."

"Is that true?"

His grin turned devilish. "Ask my mother."

They laughed for a moment. She told Tom, "Mr. Calvert sounds fine to me." To Calvert she said, "I hope you'll be happy here in Paragon Springs working with us. You didn't say if you have a wife or not. If you have family you would like to bring here, we have some nice houses that are empty, and for sale, in town."

"I might rent a house for me, I'm not married. Maybe I'll meet a nice lady here." He grinned, showing a mouthful of white teeth. He seemed to know something he wasn't saying and she guessed Tom might have told him he had proposed to her. She felt her face warm.

"Maybe you will," she said, more sternly than she intended. She added confidently, "We expect Paragon Springs to boom as word spreads about our company."

Her prophecy came true and then some over the next several months. While the new plant was being finished, and later readied for business, they sought out and hired men who would be their designers, engineers and plant managers. Most of the men were flyers, as well, whom she and Tom knew from past aviation meets. Some of them Tom had met in New York the month he worked at the Queen Aeroplane Company.

A large crew of some fifty assembly workers were hired from the community and about the county and would be trained. All of the employees were eager to be in on the ground floor of the fledgling aviation business.

"Catch The Spirit" was the theme of their advertisement being printed in newspapers and magazines around the country. Exposure in the newspapers would help their business more than anything.

Lucy Ann, though often busy on the farm, could hardly stay away from the new plant after it began operation. She managed to be there in the large cavernous building for the very first stroke of assembly of the first aeroplane. On a long line of oversized sawhorses and under the able hands of the

workers, the skeletons of aeroplane sections formed like
magic. In the air was the buzz and hum, the *feel,* of a new
miracle taking place.

She agreed to take time out when the board of health
asked her to volunteer on an investigation of a patent medicine being produced in Wichita. She went to visit the Professor Samuels Remedy Company.

The "Professor's" concoction was described in advertising as: "colorless liquid to be dropped in the eye, that
reaches every part of the body through the nerves and that
has cured and will cure practically every disease." It was
nonsense, and yet Samuels was making a small fortune from
gullible folks wracked with pain for a myriad of causes.
Many folks, believing that they couldn't afford to see a
doctor, grabbed at any cheap "cure."

Chemists Lucy Ann engaged found the eye drop cure-all
to be nothing but salt and sugar in—as she reported to the
board of health—"ordinary Wichita hydrant water."

That same month, the government authorized free
smallpox vaccine to be dispensed by the physicians of
Kansas. The authorization was the result of a year of beg-
ging from the mothers in the groups to whom she lectured.

Until she drove through Paragon Springs on her way to
the Ford County Old Settlers Picnic one Sunday late that
summer, Lucy Ann hadn't known just how much the town
was revived. Their company workers and their families had
moved into homes that had long stood boarded up and
empty. Many of the houses were fine residences that needed
only a little fixing. Children played in the yards now, women
watered flower beds, a few new automobiles sat at the curb
in front of several homes, buggies or wagons next to others.

Old businesses such as the Marble House Hotel, Wurst's

Grocery Store, Aurelia's Place Restaurant, and Jones' Drygoods, had been refurbished and looked almost new. The bakery and Murphy's boarding house had reopened. Aurelia's opera house had reopened to show moving pictures. *Moving* pictures, one more advancement she never could have imagined.

Although those who scoffed at the idea of aeroplanes as a wave of the future were still the majority, it was gratifying to know that many disbelievers were starting to believe. A good salary to pay for a nice home in a progressive town did much to convince them.

She had ordered herself a Ford automobile and another for David and Rachel. They were waiting delivery at Ham Bell's Land and Auto Company in Dodge City. Now that concrete roads were starting to be built, she thought she would get around just fine. She'd save Taffy for riding and for fieldwork.

Mr. Pickering, the blacksmith, had moved back to Missouri. If no one else decided to start up an auto company and garage in Paragon Springs, she was going to do that. Maybe Rachel and David would like to have a second business of their own, besides the farm. So far she had invested fifty thousand dollars in Paragon Springs Aviation and found she rather liked spending money.

She had bought an Edison phonograph. Although she didn't understand a word he sang, she enjoyed Enrico Caruso singing opera in *Pagliacci*. She liked other records too, especially, "On the Banks of the Wabash" and "My Old Kentucky Home."

She was singing softly, "Oh, the moonlight's fair tonight along the Wabash—" when she arrived at the fairgrounds and the Old Settlers Picnic. She drew a breath and called "Whoa" to Taffy.

★ ★ ★ ★ ★

As would be expected at such an event, there were large numbers of elderly climbing tentatively down from their rigs and autos, being led about by younger members of their families. Others, already arrived, were seated in twos and threes on benches set out especially for them.

Most of them, through hardship, had been involved in creating the county and building it up. Lucy Ann greeted those she knew, smiled and nodded at others. She wondered what the oldest of them would think of the obligatory stunt flying demonstrations later today?

Those older folk she had talked to in the recent past thought flying was unnecessary and doomed for failure. Believed that the world they worked so hard to create ought to be left alone. Well, they were wrong, and she was glad she was not so old as to believe as they did.

She moved on, sniffing the air that was rich with the fragrance of roasting beeves, a barbecuing hog or two, and frying onions and apples.

At the far edge of the grounds, fliers stood talking near the aeroplanes that would be used to give rides and demonstrate stunts. She recognized the "flying farmer" Clyde Cessna's *Silverwing* among the aeroplanes. She went over to greet her good friend whom she'd met through Tom, finding Clyde near his craft. He was dressed for flying, in jodhpurs and leather jacket. His lean face welcomed her with a smile.

"Mrs. Walsh! Good to see you! Is Tom here?"

"If he isn't already, I'm sure he will be soon."

Lately, she went out of her way not to be paired off with Tom, socially. It seemed wrong to encourage him and to give other folks the wrong idea. She felt lonely, though, as she hadn't before. Luckily, the two of them still got along comfortably talking business at the plant. Lately he had been away a lot, promoting their business. She missed him, those times, more than she thought she would.

Clyde was congratulating her on construction of the plant. "Yes," she answered him, "our company is lucky to be in high feather, doing very well. Tom works hard to promote us. Orders are coming in not just from Kansas but from other states, and a few orders from other countries. We believe we can build a plane a month in time, maybe more. Right now our employees are working ten-hour days; we don't want to work them any harder than that. If need be, we'll hire on more men."

She saw Selinda and Leonard, waved them over to meet Mr. Cessna. He agreed with Leonard that the country was suddenly "speed crazy."

"But flying can and will be practical and safe," Cessna said. "The fact that it used to make me so dizzy that I had to hold on tight to keep from falling every time that I climbed up on a thirty-five-foot windmill on the farm ought to be proof that any ordinary person can fly. Flying is different than climbing up on top of a building, where looking down makes a person dizzy."

"You must know the truth of that if anyone does, Mr. Cessna," Selinda told him with an admiring smile. "I have read that you are making one-hundred-mile flights at ninety miles an hour quite effortlessly."

"I've taken my share of spills," he reminded her, "I think I crashed eight or nine times before I got a craft to stay up for me."

He didn't mention other accidents, crashes, but Lucy Ann knew of a few. But it was like Tom said, someone had to do it, until everything about flying was known.

As Clyde had to leave them, she shook hands with him

again, and wished him good luck.

She was at a picnic table later, eating with friends and family, when she saw Tom making his way through a crowd of people across the grounds. There was a woman with him. The woman was slender, a pretty blond in a white shirt and brown jodhpurs. Her arm was laced through Tom's.

In spite of herself, Lucy Ann felt a twinge of hurt and jealousy. Which made no sense. Tom was free to have other women friends.

Chapter Nineteen

"That woman is wearing trousers!" Rachel whispered about Tom's companion. "But they're kind of attractive. I wonder who she is?"

Tom saw them, then. He waved, caught the woman's hand, and hurried over.

"Lucy Ann, friends, I'd like you to meet Sophie Albright." His eyes were glossy, his face flushed. It was as though he had had a drink too many, or was intoxicated from enjoyment of the woman's company. "Sophie is an aviatrix," he told them, "a member of the Garfield Flying Circus. I think you've seen her in action, Lucy Ann. Sophie's done her share of loop-the-loops, she's trailed sparks over nearly every little town on the prairie."

Lucy Ann remembered Sophie. Once or twice at meets she had seen her aerobatics, wing-walking, parachuting, and aeroplane to aeroplane transfer. She was a very daring young woman as well as beautiful. Lucy Ann hadn't known she was a friend of Tom's.

"It's nice to finally meet you, Sophie. I've seen you fly. Will you be performing today?"

Sophie shook her straw-colored curls. "Not today. I just came to have a good time with Tom." She turned an adoring gaze up to his face, then her pretty mouth formed a pout. "Can't fly today. I don't have my aeroplane here, my beautiful little *Bleriot*."

"Our loss," Lucy Ann nodded and smiled, while her family stared but tried to pretend that they weren't. She remembered that a favorite trick of Sophie's was to head directly at an auto on the road with her aircraft, until the auto's occupants were scared witless. Then with a flit of the tail of her craft, she would soar scores of feet above the auto.

The Garfield Flying Circus was a group of free-wheeling gypsies who often arrived in a prairie town right after harvest to take advantage of folks' fuller pockets and good spirits. But really, that was neither here nor there. Tom seemed to like her a lot.

Lucy Ann's granddaughter, Amy, prim in a white ruffled dress, had moved closer to Sophie. Amy's eyes were wide with awe as her fingers played with her bonnet strings. "You fly up in the sky in an aeroplane?" she asked in disbelief. "But you're a lady."

"I do a lot more than fly up there, sweetie," Sophie told her with a laugh, tossing her white silk scarf back over her shoulder. "In the past I danced on the stage, now I dance on the wing of my aeroplane. Maybe you'll be a flier, someday, just like me."

Amy frowned with sudden concern and shook her head. "I'm going to be a schoolteacher, like Mother."

"I'm going to be a pilot," Marcus spoke up next to Amy. His voice cracked, "I'm going to fly all over the world."

"Maybe you will and maybe you won't," Rachel said. "Right now you two need to finish your cake so we don't miss Mr. Cessna's demonstration. Don't forget he is going to toss a football out of his aeroplane, Marcus."

"I know. Zachary told me," Marcus said, climbing back onto the picnic bench and seizing his fork. He dug into his cake, took several bites, leaving chocolate crumbs around his youthful mouth.

Zachary informed them, his glance covertly on Sophie's shapely form, "Mr. Cessna is going to give five dollars to anybody who catches the football. Or, if nobody catches it direct, two dollars and fifty cents to anybody who runs after the ball and gives it back to him."

"How are the primaries looking, Leonard?" Tom asked. "The vote comes up in a few days. Are you ready to win?"

"I'm ready, but it is the voters who make the decision. I—"

"C'mon, Tom," Sophie interrupted impatiently, pulling on his arm. "I want to go where the planes are, see who we know over there besides Clyde."

"We got to go, too," Marcus said, forking cake fast.

"Yeah." Zachary finished his first, handed his mother his plate, and loped away.

"Zachary or Marcus is going to catch the football Mr. Cessna throws from the aeroplane!" Amy exclaimed, moving away from the table, her eyes enviously following her brothers. "And win five dollars!"

"Wait, you can help clean up—" Rachel started to say, but Sophie had grabbed Amy by the hand and they were racing after Zachary and Marcus. Amy looked back over her shoulder as she ran, her giggles tinged with surprise and apology.

"Well," Aurelia said, the look in her eyes bemused. "Suddenly I feel like a very old settler."

The adults around the table laughed, but Lucy Ann had been thinking approximately the same thing about herself.

It was Joey Davis who missed catching the football but scrambled after it and caught it up in his arms before anyone else. Lucy Ann reminded her grandsons that Joey likely saved their lives, there was such a collision of youngsters chasing after the ball. "And if there is something you really, really need, boys," she whispered privately,

"Grandma will give you five dollars. You, too, Amy. You can't squander it, though, mind?"

In the August primary election, Leonard lost the governor's race to Henry J. Allen by fewer than twenty votes. "He won by a hair!" Lucy Ann exclaimed after she heard and went to visit Leonard and Selinda. "It's so disappointing that you lost by just that little bit. It isn't fair."

"Funny," Leonard said with a wry smile, "but I feel like a winner. Like you say, it was a close vote. Except for Philander Winslow, who got smashed in his bid like a buffalo chip. I'm quite encouraged. I'll try again two years from now. In the meantime, it feels good to know I'll have more time to spend with my family and at my law office and at the newspaper."

"And with me," Lucy Ann said. "I'm going to need financial advice as Paragon Springs Aviation grows, as our town grows."

"You're still going to see this place turned into a great city, are you, hmm? You and my 'aunts' just won't ever give up, will you?"

Later that afternoon they all drove over in Leonard's new auto so Lucy Ann could show them the aviation plant.

Most of Tom's former farm, she pointed out, was now either grassy sod or paved landing field. "Goodbye, Russian thistle," she quipped.

Besides the air company offices, tool shops, and filling station, there were two finished hangars and another under construction besides the original barn. The hangars were built of brick, had many windows, and wide, wide doors. Inside, she showed them the neatly shelved engines, exhaust pipes, wheels, axles, carburetors, propellers along the walls, and roll after roll of canvas and silk.

As neat as a garden in the middle of the cavernous room were rows of aeroplane sections in various stages of production under the hands of workers. "It's all new," she was saying as Tom came to join them carrying a blueprint, "just a beginning, but exciting."

"Glad you're here, folks," Tom greeted Leonard and Selinda with a warm smile. "Mind if I join you?" He fell into step as they agreed and moved on. "Maybe Lucy Ann has told you that we also plan to train fliers. Besides that, and manufacture and sales, within a month or so we plan to establish an air taxi service, too."

"An air limousine?" Selinda was so astounded, the rest of them laughed.

"Exactly. Short routes at first, say between Paragon Springs, Wichita, and Kansas City. The day's not far off, though, when we'll be able to take passengers a lot farther, maybe to either coast. There will be competition, aircraft plants are cropping up all over the place, in Wichita, and in other Kansas towns. But I think there will be air business for all."

Leonard shook his head in wonder. "I have the picture. This is the *heart* right here. Outside there—" he pointed to a wide open door, "we have a strong natural south wind. Kansas is perfect for the birthplace of aviation. Glad you had the vision, Tom, you and my sister."

"Kansas is flat, too," she reminded. "You could say the entire plains is one vast natural airport. Aviation was bound to start out here somewhere."

"I'm just glad we're part of it," Tom said, smiling at her and taking her elbow as they continued their tour. He asked the others, "Did Lucy Ann tell you that we heard the other day from an oilman from over near Wichita? He said he was ready to abandon the 'crawling express trains and creeping motor cars' because they took too much time transporting him from one oil well to another. He has oil wells in the El Dorado field near Wichita, in Oklahoma and Texas, too. After he ordered one of our aeroplanes, we got orders from five of his friends. He says he will invest with us if we need him to."

Lucy Ann and Selinda were standing near a window, the men had turned back for a closer look at racks of wing frames being made on the assembly line. Selinda caught Lucy Ann's arm. "I want to apologize, Lucy Ann. Me, and a lot of others, have been wrong about you, mostly me. What you are doing here is incredible. It is obvious that Mr. Reilly knows what he's doing, too. It looks like you were the only one to see that."

"You don't have to be sorry about anything—"

"Yes, I do." Her lovely face wore a remorseful frown. "Aurelia tells me that Mr. Reilly asked you to marry him and you turned him down. If you did that because we were all so set against your having anything to do with him, we're all truly, truly sorry. We were wrong. He would make a perfect husband for you."

Now? "Oh, good heavens, Selinda! You and the others—my goodness! Dear, I made my own choices in everything, and that included whether or not to marry Tom. Had I wanted to, I would have."

"Well, I think you should change your mind. When you turned him down, you *did* make a huge mistake, Lucy Ann. I truly believe that."

Selinda, although she might not realize it, was still trying to tell her what to do. "It's too late to 'change my mind' but I don't care to, anyway."

Selinda laughed softly and put an arm around her, "Oh,

no, Lucy Ann, it is never too late, especially if you love him, and I believe you do."

She shushed Selinda as Tom and Leonard came over to them. "You know," Tom was saying, "our company can use all the publicity it can get. Would you be interested in writing us up in the *Echo*?"

"I already know the headline," Selinda told him with a nod. "It will say: TO FLY OR NOT TO FLY, THE ANSWER IS YES! We will urge our readers to drive out and examine Paragon Springs's new flying services."

Lucy Ann thought a lot about what Selinda said about changing her mind and marrying Tom. Not that she meant to, it was just interesting to explore the idea in her imagination. Married, they could talk business over breakfast, for example. They could be seen together anywhere they wanted without worrying about it. Maybe someday they would travel to Europe, by aeroplane, of course. And at night—She never got far with that particular thought. The prospect appealed, *a lot,* to her surprise, and she had to remind herself once again that she was an older woman, and was surely beyond all those exciting passions of youth. And when it came to it, if they were married, how would he really feel about that episode in her past—what the savages had done to her? He might believe it wouldn't matter. But Admire had thought that, and learned later that it did bother him.

The November 1914 election was a Republican landslide. The whole affair was exciting to Lucy Ann, even though she had voted Progressive and Leonard was not among the final candidates, having lost in the primary. Arthur Capper became Governor, and Charles Curtis U.S.

Senator. All other elected officials were Republicans. Mrs. Eva Morley Murphy from Goodland, who ran for U.S. Representative on the Progressive ticket, was not elected but did receive over 6,000 votes. A new day for women had arrived.

Lucy Ann was positive that within two years she would be voting Leonard for governor and that he would succeed.

She was dozing in front of the fire one evening in December when the phone rang, as shrill as the scream of a prairie beast, jolting her awake. *Drat the thing,* she thought. Would she ever get used to it?

Sleepily, she answered, and heard Tom's voice, calling from Wichita where he had gone on business.

"I wanted you to be one of the first to know, Lucy Ann. We got married."

"Who—did what—*what?* I can hardly hear you, Tom." She came wider awake, held the receiver tight to her ear.

"Sophie Albright and I got married," his far-off tinnish voice answered. He went on with a touch of guilt in his voice, "I'm sorry there wasn't time to invite anybody, it was sudden— Hey, would you like to talk to Sophie?"

Why on earth would she? "Yes," she mumbled, starting to feel numb, and at the same time wanting to hit something, someone, "tell her to go ahead."

"Lucy Ann," Sophie was giggling, "isn't this a surprise? We hardly knew we were going to get married, ourselves, 'til it was done. But it was such fun! We got married over Wichita in a big new *Bleriot.* The minister like to've died of fright up there. Tom and I are flying to Kansas City for a short Christmas-time honeymoon. Isn't that romantic? Lucy Ann, are you there? Tom says not to worry about the business while he's gone."

"No," she murmured, "no, I won't worry about the— business." The phone clattered as she replaced it on its hook, she staggered a bit, collapsing in her chair by the fire.

Well, what was done, was done. She had had her chance. She stared at the flames in the fireplace. She would not cry, she would not. Tears would not help at all, but, oh, it did hurt; she gasped a little, at the pain.

Chapter Twenty

It ought not to have surprised her that Tom would marry, she told herself over and over as she witnessed Tom settling his new wife into his house, his life. The marriage being so sudden, so unexpected, was what had jolted her, that still left her feeling moody and hurt. The suddenness, that's all it was that made the world seem turned upside down, and with time, she would get over it.

Of course he would be happier with a pretty young woman closer to his age. Sophie shared his passion for flying. It was true that the girl was a bit of a fluff, and reckless, but marriage would likely settle her down.

She wished them nothing but happiness, and in her heart closed the door on what might have been.

She tried not to see, in the weeks and months that followed, that marriage wasn't likely going to produce any change in Sophie. Not in a lifetime. But maybe Tom didn't really mind.

Sophie complained almost constantly that he was away too much, and she was lonely. She missed her old life with the flying circus, which had been exciting, merry sport, compared to the dull, plodding life around Paragon Springs.

When Tom was there, she complained that he spent too much time talking to Lucy Ann about business, too much time with Lucy Ann altogether.

Lucy Ann tried to be a friend, involve Sophie in the community so that she wouldn't be as lonely when Tom had to be away. But the girl wasn't interested in quilting, in Ladies Aid meetings, in teas—in making friends with the other women at all.

In addition, she had an on-running quarrel with nearly every merchant in town because they didn't carry the fashionable, up-to-date goods she felt they should stock. Anything she bought from them was of no real use to anyone but "ignorant yokels who don't know any better because they've never been anyplace else." The merchants dreaded her entry into their establishments, would just have soon done without her business than be browbeaten by her. Her petty temper-fits had become legend in a very short time.

She disliked Tom's house, it was "old, farm-ish, drab as death." But most of all she hated the town and life thereabouts.

She often went up to fly alone, took pleasure in terrifying the cows in the field by swooping down on them. It was a rare farmer around Paragon Springs who wouldn't like to grab her and shake her silly.

Lucy Ann wondered if Tom, in his absence, had any idea what he had visited on them all by marrying Sophie.

The only other bright spot for Sophie than scaring cows, when Tom was away, seemed to be Billy Calvert's good humor. She began to hang around him almost daily at the plant, stroking his tweedy lapels, laughing, teasing, sharing flying stories. They took over the office so often that Lucy Ann felt like an intruder when she needed to be there. At the same time, she wanted Sophie to be satisfied, content where she was, for Tom's sake.

She wasn't sure when she began to feel seriously uneasy about Sophie's attitude toward Paragon Springs and the business. But as days passed the young woman's many whimpers and dissatisfactions became like sand, building into gigantic unpleasant piles of complaint, that threatened to smother everything.

She tried not to worry. Their factory was well-launched. They twice had to hire more workers to fill the many orders for aeroplanes.

After flying demonstrations at the Old Settlers Picnic last summer, and Selinda and Leonard's visit to the new aviation plant, the *Tri-County Echo* had stated, "As soon as the wheat crop is in, the farmers and ranchers will be flying high, every one of them will want an aeroplane."

It had turned out to be a fairly accurate statement. That story had been picked up by the *Kansas City Star* and then reprinted around the nation. Paragon Springs Aviation Company was the plant mentioned as the one to contact.

Their newest design underway was a three-place, tandem-cockpit biplane. It would carry a pilot, two passengers and baggage, and would fly more than two hundred miles without landing.

Lucy Ann went to the plant's main office one day to discuss the hiring of more pilot-salesmen and walked directly into a heated, three-way argument between Tom, Sophie, and Billy Calvert.

Billy was redfaced and for once he wasn't grinning. "It's exactly what ought to be done!" he was telling Tom as he gripped the back of a chair.

Tom, looking somehow cornered as he stood by a shelf of papers, ran a hand through his hair in agitation. "I know you two think so, but I don't believe—"

"You'll be sorry your whole life if you don't, Tom Reilly!" Sophie's voice was full of fury as she swung back and forth in front of Tom's desk. While Lucy Ann watched,

Sophie petulantly shoved a basket of papers off the desk onto the floor.

Tom saw Lucy Ann then, and his look of worry turned to crimson-faced embarrassment.

She said quickly,"Excuse me, I didn't mean to break in on you all—I'll come back later."

"No, Lucy Ann, don't leave," Tom held out a hand. "Come on in. You're involved in this, too."

A nervous shiver traveled her spine. "What's wrong? You all look a bit discombobulated."

"Tom," Sophie said, with a glaring look at Lucy Ann, "you can do what you want. This is your factory, too. Just tell her you want to leave—"

Alarm ricocheted through Lucy Ann, stilled her heart. "Leave?" She looked at Tom for an explanation.

His eyes flashed confusion, anger. "My wife, here, and Billy, think Paragon Springs is the wrong place for an aviation plant. They want to move it."

She was sure she hadn't heard right. "Move it?" she asked through a dry throat, incredulous. "But we're doing fine! We've only gotten started, we're just starting to expand." What they were saying was so ridiculous she had to wonder if this was one of Billy's jokes. But from the look on their faces this was serious talk. They meant it. Her knees went weak, her mind went numb.

"You may think this plant is big stuff," Sophie spoke to her as though she were an ignorant, backwoods child. "The company is nothing to what it could be—if we combined with say, the Wichita Aircraft Company in Wichita. Or Glenn Curtiss's company out in California. There is money, and oil, around Wichita, it isn't a backward hick town like Paragon Springs. And California, if we moved the plant there—"

Propped on her hands, Sophie leaned back against the desk. She had the audacity to smile sympathetically at Lucy Ann. She looked suddenly confident that her dream would happen and there was nothing Lucy Ann could do to stop it. The anger in her pretty face slowly melted and her eyes shone.

"No, the plant will not be moved." Lucy Ann stood stiffly, her heart frozen like a rock with fear. This foolish young woman with her silly whims could destroy what it had taken other women and their friends forty-odd years to build. She couldn't let her do that. Yank the plant away, like the bottom of a house of cards, bringing it all down flat. She cleared her throat, "Tom, how do you feel about this?"

He looked away; her heart sank as he said grimly from the corner of his mouth, "We can talk about it later, Lucy Ann, I just wanted them to hear your opinion, direct from you." He looked fed up, at wit's end, and for the moment, helpless.

She wanted to talk about it right then. Straighten it out that the plant would stay. That over her dead body was the only way a brick or aeroplane of it would be moved. "All right, Tom," she said finally, "we can talk later. But I ask you all to remember that I have a lot invested in this plant, I am an equal partner."

She stood straighter. "Please remember that there are over two hundred people who have moved here because of the plant, and they are happy here. Think of them and their children," she said huskily, "they wouldn't want to move again. This is not a time to give up. As the plant grows, the town and its conveniences will grow. Paragon Springs will eventually be able to offer everything anyone could ask for. The future is here, for me. I hope it will be for the three of you." She turned and left.

★ ★ ★ ★ ★

Tom came by her house that evening. She had waited for him on pins and needles. She had put her supper in the icebox, untouched, for lack of appetite.

"Sophie doesn't like it here," he explained after they sat down at her kitchen table with coffee. "Not the town, not my place, not the people."

"I've seen that."

"She wants to leave, and she wants me to go with her. If I don't, she says our marriage is over." He poured cream in his coffee, his hand seemed to shake when he stirred it with a spoon.

She sighed heavily. It was as she suspected. With one little tug of Tom's heartstrings, Sophie could ruin everything the women of Paragon Springs and their loved ones had spent a lifetime building. One small woman who wanted her own way could destroy it all, with marital blackmail.

With her eyes steady on Tom's face she said, "You'll have to make up your mind yourself, Tom. If you decide to leave, I will buy you out, but the plant stays."

"How will you run it?" *Without me,* his eyes were asking.

"I don't know. You had the dream, you are the brains behind Paragon Springs Aviation even though it was my idea to have the plant here and I have provided money, and the will. Somehow, I'll figure out how to keep it running, but I won't let this company end, here, before it is hardly begun. And that is my final word."

"I need to think about it some more. Of course I don't want to leave. We've invested a fortune. And I made you a promise when we decided to build the plant that it would be here, and nowhere else. I want to keep that promise. But Sophie is my wife. I made a pledge to her, too, when I married her. As her husband, I owe her happiness, and she wants to leave. The sooner the better."

She shrugged. It was hard to find her voice. "It's up to you, Tom. I don't want to see you leave. But if you feel you must, I'll understand. But the plant doesn't budge an inch."

Two weeks later, while Tom was still trying to determine the best thing to do, Billy Calvert and Sophie ran off together.

Word drifted back that they had tried to make themselves part of a new Wichita aviation company, Laird's, but were rejected. They then went to California where they were taken on at an aviation plant there.

A month after that, Tom got a letter from Sophie asking for a divorce. She was in love with Billy, she said, he was fun, and they wanted to marry. California, she wrote, was all they dreamed of, and the best thing she ever did in her life was to leave Kansas.

"I would guess she adds me to Kansas when she says the best thing she ever did was leave," Tom told Lucy Ann ruefully as they sat talking in the company office one day. He looked older than before his marriage, haggard and worn, his eyes shadowed with sadness. "I knew almost as soon as I married Sophie that I had made a huge mistake. But she was so beautiful, so daring to watch, and she loved to fly. She turned me into a fool-headed, love-sick idiot. I guess I thought that was plenty for marriage, but turns out it's not."

She nodded, remained silent to allow him to talk. She could hardly imagine his pain, but she knew it had to be great. A heart taken lightly could near destroy a person.

She felt partly responsible for his trouble. She had

turned him down awful blunt and quick when he had asked her to marry him. Maybe that had something to do with him rushing into something with Sophie that wasn't the best for either of them.

He thumped the desk hard with his knuckle, making an inkwell bounce. "She had me so blinded I had no trouble at all overlooking her faults. She had them aplenty," he said with a bark of a laugh, that was closer to tears than humor. "Lord, what a mistake I made! Stupidest thing I've done since I allowed myself to be blown out of a cannon that time."

They both laughed.

He finished in a hollow voice, "Well, I hope she and Billy will be happy. They deserve each other."

"You'll be all right?" She reached across a stack of papers to touch his hand.

"Yes." He drew a long breath, chin tucked in his collar, then he curled his fingers around hers. "I will be." His grin was twisted. "The strong survive, don't they say? But I want to go away a while and shake this off, and I need your approval."

She squeezed his hand, continued to hold on to it. "Heavens to Betsy, you don't need my sayso for wanting to get away a while."

"For this, I do. This is for the company, too. And you are part of the company."

"Explain." It was hard to concentrate, her feelings were in such a twirl from his closeness, from his pain that she wanted to ease, but she forced herself to mind what he had to tell her.

"I want to go to Paris. Study what the French are accomplishing in aviation. They were 'way ahead of the United States with manufacture of the *Bleriot*, they are

212

ahead of us still. We could duplicate the best of their designs on our next line of planes. What do you think?" His
deep frown began to smooth out, the look in his eyes became a trifle clearer, more like his old self.

He was going to be all right then, like he said, given
time. "I think it is a wonderful plan." She scooted her office
chair around close beside his at the desk until her shoulder
touched his. He moved some blueprints and other papers
and opened a notebook. "We will have to hire more special-
ists," she said.

He agreed. "Billy has to be replaced."

She moved a bottle of ink closer and took up an ink pen.
He took up another and passed her a second notebook. She
hesitated just for a moment, loving him with her eyes, and
told him, "You know, nothing grows in Kansas without
care and cultivation, and never did."

As he caught her double meaning, he looked the hap-
piest, the most satisfied, she had seen him look, ever. He
drew her into his arms and kissed her, a kiss that surely
lasted a full two minutes, until she was breathless, and then,
he kissed her again.

Later, with heads together, they began to draw Paragon
Springs's future, and their own, for all enduring time.

About the Author

Irene Bennett Brown has known she wanted to write since age thirteen when she read *Little Women*. After listening to the many stories of her older family members about the early times in Kansas, she determined to tell the story of the role women and children played in developing the West.

She has written several young adult books, including *Before the Lark*, winner of the Spur Award and nominee for the Mark Twain Award. Her first adult novel, *The Plainswoman*, was widely acclaimed and nominated for the Spur Award.

Brown lives in Oregon with her husband, Bob.

The employees of Five Star hope you have enjoyed this book. All our books are made to last. Other Five Star books are available at your library, through selected bookstores, or directly from us.

For information about titles, please call:

(800) 223-1244

or visit our Web site at:

www.gale.com/fivestar

To share your comments, please write:

Publisher
Five Star
295 Kennedy Memorial Drive
Waterville, ME 04901